"We're pretending to be tourists tonight."

He turned and lifted a long white box off the table. "This is for you. A disguise."

Glory accepted the box. In it was a lei that featured a variety of flowers in hues of red, white and pink woven together with delicate fronds of fern.

"Thank you," she said. "Will you put it on for me?"

Jared knew the custom. He had given Glory the lei, but the ritual wouldn't be complete until he slipped it over her head. He was curiously reluctant to perform the simple act.

His palms grazed her cheeks as he lowered the wreath over her head, and he leaned forward to brush a kiss on her forehead. He wanted to linger there, to taste her again, to feel her arms slide around his waist to hold him. He wanted...

Dear Reader,

Welcome to Silhouette—experience the magic of the wonderful world where two people fall in love. Meet heroines who will make you cheer for their happiness, and heroes (be they the boy next door or a handsome, mysterious stranger) who will win your heart. Silhouette Romance reflects the magic of love—sweeping you away with books that will make you laugh and cry, heartwarming, poignant stories that will move you time and time again.

In the coming months we're publishing romances by many of your all-time favorites, such as Diana Palmer, Brittany Young, Sondra Stanford and Annette Broadrick. Your response to these authors and our other Silhouette Romance authors has served as a touchstone for us, and we're pleased to bring you more books with Silhouette's distinctive medley of charm, wit and—above all—*romance*.

I hope you enjoy this book and the many stories to come. Experience the magic!

Sincerely,

Tara Hughes
Senior Editor
Silhouette Books

EMILIE RICHARDS

Island Glory

Published by Silhouette Books New York
America's Publisher of Contemporary Romance

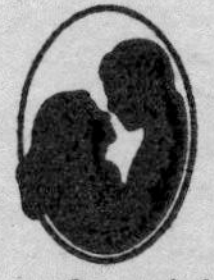

SILHOUETTE BOOKS
300 E. 42nd St., New York, N.Y. 10017

ISBN: 0-373-08675-X

First Silhouette Books printing September 1989

Printed in the U.S.A.

Books by Emilie Richards

Silhouette Romance

Brendan's Song #372
Sweet Georgia Gal #393
Gilding the Lily #401
Sweet Sea Spirit #413
Angel and the Saint #429
Sweet Mockingbird's Call #441
Good Time Man #453
Sweet Mountain Magic #466
Sweet Homecoming #489
Aloha Always #520
Outback Nights #536
Island Glory #675

Silhouette Intimate Moments

Lady of the Night #152
Bayou Midnight #188
**From Glowing Embers* #249
**Smoke Screen* #261
**Rainbow Fire* #273
**Out of the Ashes* #285

Silhouette Special Edition

All the Right Reasons #433
A Classic Encounter #456

* Tales of the Pacific series

EMILIE RICHARDS

believes that opposites attract, and her marriage is vivid proof. "When we met," the author says, "the *only* thing my husband and I could agree on was that we were very much in love. Fortunately, we haven't changed our minds about that in all the years we've been together."

The couple lives in Ohio with their four children, who span from toddler to teenager. Emilie has put her master's degree in family development to good use—raising her own brood, working for Head Start, counseling in a mental-health clinic and serving in VISTA.

Though her first book was written in snatches with an infant on her lap, Emilie now writes five hours a day and "rejoices in the opportunity to create, to grow and to have such a good time."

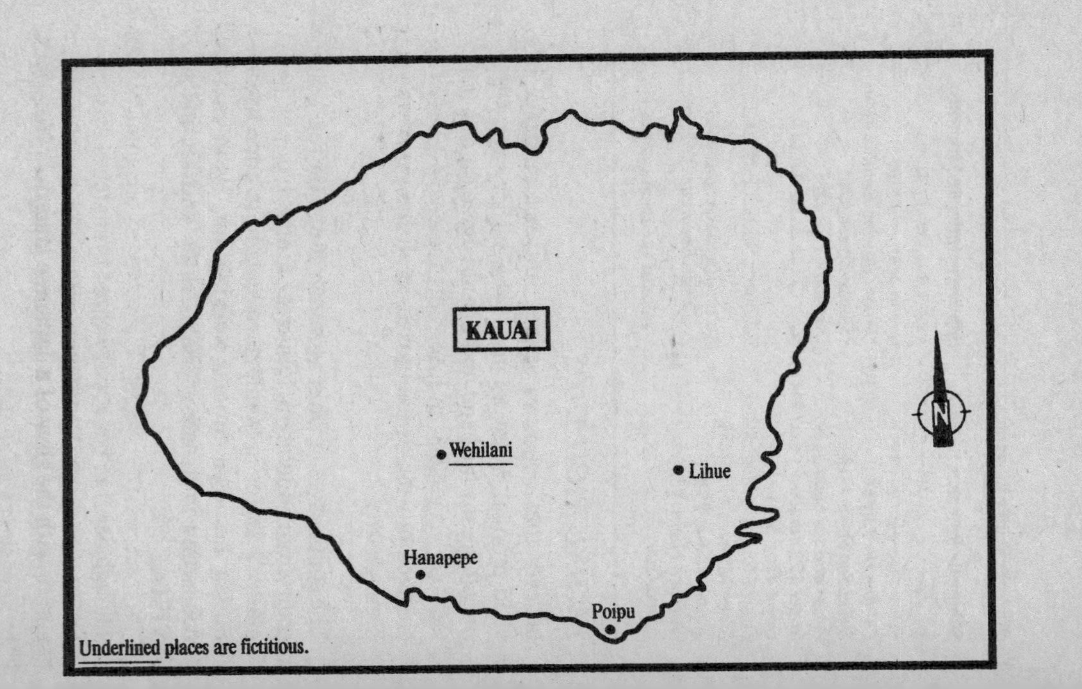
KAUAI
Wehilani
Lihue
Hanapepe
Poipu
N
Underlined places are fictitious.

Chapter One

Miss?"

The butler, a tall man of Oriental extraction who was built like a sumo wrestler, smiled in a way that was becoming all too familiar to Glory. The smile radiated sympathy.

Glory Kalia smiled, too, as if she understood the unspoken condolences that had made her first week as manager of Wehilani the strangest seven days of her life. "May I help you, Paradox?"

"I was just about to leave for the weekend, miss. Was there anything you needed down below?"

Down below. Glory thought just how apt that description was. Not *in town*. Just *down below*. Three thousand feet down below, accessible only by helicopter, horseback or one long hike.

"Some sunshine, maybe?" she mused out loud. "Mangoes? Hibiscus? Pretty girls in bikinis?"

Paradox unleashed a brighter smile. For a moment it lit the room with the glow of a Japanese lantern. "Homesick, miss?"

She considered that possibility. Then she shook her head. "Lonely. Before you leave, you wouldn't want to tell me what the staff finds so peculiar about my being here, would you?" She asked the question with no malice. She simply wanted to know why the entire staff—Paradox; Sally, the housekeeper; her husband Rolfe, the grounds keeper; and One Leg, the stableman—were keeping something from her. Until they let her in on their secret, she had no friends in this remote spot where friends could be important.

"Peculiar?" Paradox made an obvious effort to pretend he didn't know what she meant.

Glory could see that Paradox's ruse held no malice, either. But apparently the secret was impossible to share. "You don't want to tell me what's going on? I might be able to help."

Paradox seemed to weigh the question. Glory wasn't sure if he shook his head or if he just needed to flex his massive neck. One thing was clear: he had no intention of telling her anything.

Glory was discouraged, but she didn't allow it to show. Who could argue with a man who looked like Oddjob, the shiny-pated hat thrower who had been James Bond's nemesis in *Goldfinger*?

"There's nothing I can get for you down below?" Paradox repeated.

"Nothing. Have a nice weekend, Paradox."

"Mahalo." For just a second, he looked as if he wanted to say something more revealing than a Hawaiian thank-you. Then he nodded. "By the time I come back Monday night, miss, Mr. Farrell will already be here."

"I know. Everything will be ready for him."

"Just so." He sighed. "Everything." He turned and left the room with the peculiar grace of a man who has spent decades learning to keep his bulk from destroying the immediate environment.

He left the door ajar, but that didn't bother Glory. No one would disturb her. Her office was in the west wing of the Farrell manor, flanked by rooms that hadn't been used since she had come to Wehilani, a vast mountain estate on the island of Kauai. On one side there was a mahogany-paneled library stocked with leather-bound volumes of classics, on the other a lace-draped, gold-leaf adorned lady's parlor, although there was no lady in attendance. Across the hall there was a conservatory filled with carefully tended potted palms and ferns that made her think of a funeral parlor.

The west wing smelled of furniture polish, potting soil and the subtler odor of disuse. There were no cobwebs hanging like ghostly watchmen in the hallway, no creaking floorboards, but the west wing, like the rest of the house, seemed haunted by an absence of footsteps and laughter.

Glory realized she was staring at nothing and pulled her gaze back to her office. In direct contrast to the other rooms, the office was uncluttered and modern. It hadn't been that way when she arrived. Her predecessor had been an old man who had apparently reveled in the well-bred gloom of the other rooms. Every available inch of the office floor had been covered with ornate furniture; every available inch of wall space had been covered with oil paintings of the American West.

Now the paintings decorated the walls of a second-story guest room, and the mahogany furniture graced its floor. In their places Glory had installed comfortable wicker that she had found gathering dust in the attic and adorned the walls with scavenged watercolors of Wehilani, painted by one of the original Farrells. The most spectacular difference, however, was the windows. Where three layers of heavy fabric had successfully blocked the Hawaiian sunshine, there was now only squeaky-clean glass. When the sun shone, it would flood the small room and wash away the west-wing gloom with a torrent of light.

When the sun shone.

The drone of Jared Farrell's personal helicopter closed in on the heliport behind the east wing. Glory realized that Paradox's ride into sunshine had arrived. She rose to walk to the windows and look out over the miles of green that led to a blue sea she could just glimpse through a gap in the neighboring mountains. The sun hadn't really shone since she had arrived. They were in the clouds. Wehilani was the Hawaiian word for "heavenly adornment."

In the past week she'd had to forcibly remind herself that she was still living in the Hawaiian islands. Kauai wasn't so terribly different from its sister island, Oahu, where Glory had spent all of her twenty-two years. So why did this place seem so strange? And why, for the first time in her life, was she lonely?

A faint chuckle brightened the room as Glory realized how funny that was. She was one of six children. As she'd grown up, privacy had been a commodity no one dared cherish, and loneliness had been an impossibility. Perhaps because of her background, she had leaped at this chance for peace, space and serenity. When Toby and Cole Chandler, her employers at the Aikane Hotel, had told her that their friend, the inventor Jared Farrell, was interviewing candidates to manage his estate and that they had recommended her, the opportunity had seemed so perfect, she had almost been afraid to hope.

Because Mr. Farrell was in Europe, Glory's grueling job interview had been conducted by Hugh Glenreigh, the old man whom she was replacing. She had been one of a dozen candidates, and despite Toby and Cole's references, she hadn't believed the job would be hers.

Astonishingly, she had been hired to start work immediately, although she still hadn't met Jared Farrell. Except for the information in two newspaper articles she had found in a Honolulu library, she knew little about him. The articles had called him a mystery and hinted that he marched to a different drummer. Among other things, he had created a device that improved the fuel economy of automobiles by twenty percent. He was purported to be wealthy beyond imagination, handsome as sin and elusive as Wehilani sunshine. On the other hand, Toby and Cole, who knew him well, claimed he was a sensitive, compassionate genius who just happened to have inherited one-fifth of Kauai. But even they refused to tell Glory more than that, insisting that she must make her own judgment.

So, strangely enough, here she was with a boss she hadn't met, a staff that clucked their tongues in sympathy every time she passed, and the management of a magnificent mausoleum perched so high in the clouds it might have been Jack's bean stalk destination.

"He aha hou a'e?" she murmured out loud, choosing the colorful Hawaiian version of the universal "What's next?"

As if in answer there was a crash in back of her, unquestionably the sound of the office door hitting the wall behind it. Then a voice.

"Who the hell let *you* in here?"

The helicopter's lift-off had masked every other sound. Glory hadn't heard anyone approach. Now she took her time turning toward the outraged tones resonating from the doorway.

She considered the man's question as she examined him. He was a good eight inches taller than her own five-three, broad shouldered and lean. She couldn't say for sure what his superbly tailored gray suit was hiding, but she would bet her life that his trim physique was defined by muscle. This dark-haired, blazing-eyed man was no office-bound bureaucrat with soft hands and manicured nails. The newspaper photograph she had seen hadn't done him justice, but this was undeniably Jared Farrell, her new boss. And he looked as tough as the words he had spoken.

Glory, on the other hand, with her short skirt, aloha shirt and hair falling free to her hips, knew she looked like a teenage hula dancer at the Ala Moana mall. She had only one way to show this man she was mature enough to perform the job she'd been hired to do. She lifted her chin slightly and straightened her shoulders.

"I'm sorry," she said softly, refusing to be intimidated. "Were you by any chance swearing at me?"

Jared was nearly dead on his feet. He had just made an exhausting trip halfway across the world, and all he really wanted was a firm mattress, Wehilani serenity and twenty-four hours of sleep. He did not want a confrontation with the woman he'd almost married, the woman who had lied to him months before with every swish of her curvaceous hips and every flirtatious blink of her velvet-black eyes.

He didn't know what Patsy Hightower was doing in his manager's office, but as he watched her turn to answer his question, he swiftly planned just how he was going to get rid of her. There was only one way. Summoning his private helicopter again would take too long. She would have to go down the mountain on horseback, preferably on Goblin, a nag with a trot that rattled like a jackhammer.

The woman by the window was fully facing him and speaking before Jared realized his mistake. She was an island woman, too, one of the exceptionally beautiful wahines that only Hawaii seemed to produce. Her face reflected a mixture of proud heritages: Polynesian, Caucasian and Oriental. The Polynesian was evident in the suntanned hue of her skin and the thick cascade of waving jet-black hair; the Caucasian in her narrow nose and delicate bones; the Oriental in the tilt of her huge dark eyes. The combination added up to a startling whole. She was breathtaking.

And she was not Patsy Hightower.

"No, I wasn't swearing at *you*," Jared answered, still examining her.

Glory smiled just a little. "I'm always jumping to conclusions."

He noted the musical lilt of her voice. It was one of the ways she was different from Patsy. Patsy's voice was low and sultry, the steamy heat of a tropical summer's night. This woman's was sweeter, higher—a spring evening with the scent of plumeria and the sound of the ocean on the soft warm breeze.

Her mouth was different, too. Patsy's was full-lipped and pouting. This woman's was softer, innocent—if such a word could apply to something so provocative—and definitely not pouting. Right now it was turned up slightly at the corners, and he had a gut-level instinct that it stayed that way more often than not. She saw the world as a humorous place.

Her sort of innocent allure was more dangerous than all of Patsy's calculations.

"I'll rephrase my question," Jared said, forcing the fury from his voice. "What are you doing in here?" For the first time his gaze left and traveled around the office. "And what happened to all the furniture?"

"I'm in here because I'm the new manager." She waited for him to introduce himself. When he didn't, she refused to acknowledge that she knew who he was. "And the furniture and paintings are up in the smallest guest room on the second floor." She couldn't resist an addition. "It'll be a perfect place to entertain cowboys."

"Some of those paintings were Remingtons and Russells."

She held up her hands in a display of innocence. "Not a horse was scratched."

"Your name?"

A flutter of anger passed through her at his rudeness. She quelled it. "Glory Kalia."

"Glory's your real name?"

She heard the disbelief in his voice. "Believe me, I didn't wish it on myself. I was the first girl in the family. When I was born my mother's first words were 'Glory hallelujah.'"

"And is your middle name Hallelujah?"

"The name on my birth certificate's actually Kololia, the Hawaiian equivalent of Glory. My parents thought Kololia Kalia was enough to saddle me with. I've appreciated that."

Jared wondered if her parents had known that their dark-haired little baby girl would turn out to personify the name they had given her. He wondered how many men had already fallen victim to her glorious charms. "Do you know who I am?"

Glory shook her head, and a yard-long lock of hair slid over her shoulder to caress her breast. "You've neglected to tell me."

"I'm Jared Farrell."

She wondered if he expected her to faint from horror. "I suspected as much." She walked toward him, extending her hand politely. "I'm sorry I wasn't at the front door to greet you, but I was told you weren't arriving until Monday."

Jared considered ignoring her hand. He didn't want to shake it; he didn't want to touch her. He compromised by just grasping her slender fingers, then dropping them quickly. "Miss Kalia, I telephoned Sally this morning to let her know to expect me today. Obviously a practical joke's been played on us both."

She was surprised at the warm touch of a man whose scowl could freeze the Atlantic. "I'm not sure how practical it was, Mr. Farrell. It seems to have gotten us off on the wrong foot."

He didn't want to stand in the doorway any longer. His sigh was like the hiss of air from a deflating tire. "Look, I've been flying for what seems like days. I need food, a change of clothes, sleep."

"Shall I find Sally and have her prepare lunch for you while you change?"

He shook his head in frustration. "No. I don't want to wait for anything. I'm going to my suite. I'll make myself something. We'll talk..." His eyes focused on the lock of hair still snaking provocatively across her breast. He'd been about to say "later." He changed his mind. He wasn't going to let Glory Kalia stay at Wehilani one moment longer than necessary. "There. Now."

Jared Farrell's suite was the only part of Wehilani that Glory still hadn't explored. She knew the rest of the house and the immediate grounds as well as she knew the Aikane Hotel, but she hadn't felt comfortable exploring Jared's private rooms. Now she had her chance.

"Fine," she said. "Perhaps you'll let me put some lunch together for you while you change."

"You weren't hired to cook for me, Miss Kalia."

"I'm aware of that, but I've never refused to help a weary traveler." She smiled to show she was more reasonable than he was.

Jared's long sigh continued as if it hadn't been interrupted by conversation. Then he turned and started down the corridor.

Aristocratic, ill-tempered, in need of work on his manners, and altogether as "different" as the newspaper articles had hinted. Glory ticked off Jared's most visible qualities as she followed silently behind him. Long legged, handsomer than sin—if you ignored the scowl—and remarkably upset about something.

She had a feeling she was about to find out why the rest of the staff had been shaking their heads all week.

Jared stalked the wide hallways as if he were a man with a mission. He climbed the gray marble staircase and turned into the east wing, where his suite was located. His rooms were at the far end of the corridor, as far from house traffic as they could be. They were undeniably his hideaway. He turned once to see if Glory had kept up with him.

She had, and the image of her petite body clothed in a hip-hugging white skirt with a lavender Hawaiian-print blouse was enough to make him turn back to his mission with more determination. She had the natural grace, the fluid dancer stride, of many island women. She had twisted her hip-length hair into a knot as she walked, and when he had glimpsed her, she had been anchoring it on top of her head with what looked like ivory chopsticks. The vision of her, arms raised in that surprisingly seductive pose, nipped at him as he continued to the corridor's end.

He had caught her off guard, and now, with no seeming embarrassment, she was assuming a more professional appearance. He wondered what she would have worn if she'd known he was coming. A gabardine suit?

It wouldn't have mattered. She was a woman who couldn't disguise her delicate feminine beauty no matter what she wore—or didn't. Not for the first time he asked himself how Hugh Glenreigh, the estate manager who had served Wehilani well for so many years, could have been foolish enough to hire a replacement who looked like Glory Kalia.

When the answer came, it was as clear as Glory's midnight eyes. Hugh had done it on purpose!

Jared muttered a string of expletives that would have turned Glory's ears blue if she could have distinguished them. All she heard was audible anger. She wondered if he often swore to himself this way. Handsome as sin and comfortable indulging in it, too.

Jared threw his door open, then stepped aside to let Glory pass ahead. She was faintly surprised. She wasn't a servant, but she was Jared's employee. She hadn't expected this show of good manners, especially not after their interactions so far. She passed in front of him, brushing lightly against his suit coat as she did.

As she passed, Jared inhaled the scent of fresh air and mountain woodlands. He had expected the cloying fragrance that Patsy had worn, a heavy-handed attempt to translate Hawaii's rich floral heritage into perfume. But even if the two women's choices of scents were different, he doubted that their differences extended much deeper.

Glory was certainly younger and less obviously marked by greed and vanity than Patsy, but he'd known enough beautiful women to realize that Glory must know where her charms lay. Youth, freshness, innocence, vulnerability. She played on her attributes like young David on his harp. Later, when youth was a fading memory, she would undoubtedly develop Patsy's predatory gleaming eyes, her feral, toothy smile.

But she wouldn't be at Wehilani, so he wouldn't have to watch it happen.

Glory stood in a small foyer and waited for Jared to close the door. His suite was really a large apartment, utterly private and self-contained. To her right she could see a small well-equipped kitchen, to her left a large room furnished with a desk, a drafting table and a huge worktable flanked by tall shelves of books and a variety of implements ranging from common carpenters' tools to laboratory equipment.

"Straight ahead, Miss Kalia." Glory felt Jared touch her shoulder to move her down the hallway. She obliged him, wondering what else there was to see.

Jared watched the fascinated way Glory examined everything she saw. Patsy had shown the same degree of interest. Of course, now he understood that Patsy had just been adding up his net worth. He imagined she had figured it almost to the penny.

"Were you expecting tortured monkeys in cages?" he asked dryly.

"Not really, but frankly, I'm relieved there's no assistant named Igor, no weird violin music."

"Most of my work space is in the laboratory behind the house."

"Which needs a thorough cleaning."

Jared flinched. "No one goes in that building, Miss Kalia. Not to clean, not to inspect."

"I haven't been inside," she assured him, stepping into a spacious living room. Unlike the rest of the house, this room was sparsely furnished with contemporary teak upholstered with Haitian cotton. The paintings gracing the stark white walls were impressionistic scenes of Kauai. There were no curtains on the windows.

"This is lovely," she said, turning to smile at Jared.

He met her smile with a frown. "If you didn't go inside, Miss Kalia, then how did you know my laboratory was in need of a good cleaning?"

"There are windows. Dirty windows," she added. "I was told my job here was to manage all aspects of the estate, so I've spent the last week inspecting the house and immediate grounds and acquainting myself with everything."

Jared motioned Glory toward a chair. She shook her head. "I meant what I said about making you something to eat while you change. Do you have any preferences?"

Jared ran a weary hand through his dark hair. He wanted this confrontation over with. He also wanted a shower.

Perhaps the second would give him the strength for the first. "Thank you," he said at last. "I don't care what you fix."

She nodded, then started down the hall toward the kitchen.

Jared took his time in the shower. The warm water soaked through the first layer of his weariness so that by the time he emerged, he was almost ready to confront Glory.

She was waiting for him in the living room, where she'd set out a platter of fresh fruit, cheese and crackers and a pot of tea. "Your kitchen needs stocking," she said, turning from the window where she had been gazing out at the ocean. It was clearly visible here and eased her homesickness.

The sight of Jared, fresh from the shower, clad in snug jeans so faded they were almost white and an oxford shirt with sleeves rolled up to reveal his tanned forearms, eased nothing at all. The casual clothing emphasized his sharply hewn features and elegantly rangy frame to remind her that he was a man, as well as her boss. And he was a man to be reckoned with.

"Sit down, Miss Kalia." Jared motioned her to a chair beside the sofa where he had already seated himself. He watched the graceful sway of her body as she moved across the room and lowered herself into the chair.

Glory leaned over to reach for the teapot to pour him a cup. "This should be steeped by now."

Jared stopped her with his hand on top of hers. His fingers brushed across her skin, and his eyes followed them. Her hand was small and long fingered, with shapely, unadorned nails. She wore a simple white coral bracelet on her wrist but no other jewelry. She emphasized her innocence well. He withdrew his hand.

"I don't want you waiting on me," he said firmly. "I brought you here to discuss your employment."

Glory sat back, meeting his gaze. "All right."

"There's been a mistake," he began. He stopped, examining what he'd just said and began again. "That's not quite true. It's a mistake, all right, but no mistake was made."

Her mouth curved up in an unintentional smile. He wasn't making any sense at all. Probably not even to himself.

Jared muttered something under his breath and leaned over to pour his tea, stopping before a drop left the pot. "You didn't get yourself a cup," he said.

"I didn't know we were having tea together."

He muttered something else and stood to stride down the hall. He returned a minute later with a cup for Glory. "Pour."

She obliged him, filling his, too. She watched him raise it to his lips. He looked as if he wished the tea were something stronger. "A mistake?" she asked when he'd drained half his cup.

Jared leaned back against the sofa cushions and closed his eyes for a moment, his cup balanced against his thigh. He wanted nothing more than just to have this over with. "Hugh Glenreigh's mistake, only it wasn't a mistake at all."

"I begin to see." Glory hid her smile against her teacup.

Jared opened his eyes and glared at her. "I'll stop beating around the bush. Hugh hired you to spite me."

There was no more need for a teacup to hide anything. Glory lowered it to her lap. She was no longer smiling. "Would you please explain?"

"Let's just say that Hugh had a mind of his own. When it came time for him to retire, he didn't want to. He and his wife had been at Wehilani for most of their married life. She died about four years ago. After that, Hugh seemed to lose his strength and zest for living. He wasn't as attentive to details—" he saw Glory nod as if she had figured that out in her week at the estate "—and he began to make mistakes that were both costly and, occasionally, dangerous. He wasn't taking care of his health, and I began to worry that he might need immediate medical attention one day and that we'd lose him before we could get him off the mountain. So I told him he had to leave."

Jared stared into space as if he were reviewing that decision. "He's sixty-eight," he said. "He has three children on the island and grandchildren galore. His daughter's been after him to move in with her since their mother died. When I finally approached her about Hugh, she encouraged me to force him to retire."

Glory noted the goodwill that radiated through Jared's explanation. But she was more interested in something else. "What does this have to do with me?"

"Hugh wasn't happy about having to leave. I wanted him to know I still respected him, so up until the day he left, I gave him as much responsibility as usual. When I found I was going to have to be in Athens for most of this month, I asked him to hire his own replacement."

"I still don't see the problem."

"Miss Kalia, I gave Hugh a list of requirements. I told him I wanted a man, thirty-five or older, someone who was looking for a permanent position and wouldn't be off looking for greener pastures after a month or two of Wehilani's isolation. Look at yourself. You don't fit that description, do you?"

Glory felt anger rising inside her. She usually cut anger off at its point of origin, having learned long ago in the inevitable fights with her siblings that showing emotion was as good as handing them a victory. Serenity was a sharper weapon and more her style. Now style flew out the window.

She set her cup carefully on the table, but her hand was trembling. "There are qualifications you just forgot to mention, though I'm sure you mentioned them to Hugh. Experience, suitability and desire for the job. Outstanding references."

"Those go without saying."

"Only to someone who didn't think they were important."

Jared's eyes narrowed. "There's nothing insulting about the truth, Miss Kalia. You're a beautiful young woman, and beautiful young women are usually looking for handsome young men. You won't find one at Wehilani."

She struggled not to blanket him in her fury. She breathed in deeply, her nostrils flaring with the effort. When she finally spoke, she sounded calm although she was still seething inside. "I want to be sure I have this straight when I speak to my attorney, Mr. Farrell. Your employee hired me at your request. But now you find me unsuitable for the position because of my age, my sex and my beauty?"

Jared knew just where she was heading. "If you think—"

"And while we're at it, why not go for broke? What about my family tree?" she continued. "Do you find that unsuitable, too? Was Hugh told not to hire someone of Hawaiian descent? After all, your ancestors made it perfectly clear how they felt about mine!"

For a moment Jared couldn't believe he had heard her clearly. Then he slammed his cup on the table, ignoring the sound of china splintering as he leaned toward her. "Are you accusing me of prejudice, Miss Kalia?"

She leaned forward to meet him. Her eyes didn't waver. "Yes. I am. Now *you* tell me all the forms it's taken."

Jared stared into her unblinking eyes. He gathered every ounce of self-control he possessed to keep from wrapping his fingers around her throat and remained silent.

Glory saw his fury, and she saw something more as he mastered it. A dawning awareness of his guilt.

"Prejudice," she said softly when they had stared at each other for more than a minute. "To prejudge another on the basis of some irrelevant detail such as age or sex or appearance." She hesitated. "Or ethnic background," she said at last.

He ignored the first three, because both of them knew she was right, and addressed the fourth. "Wehilani is a small United Nations. How can you look at the staff here and accuse me of racism?"

"There are no Hawaiians."

Part of Jared's success had come from his ability to know when to quit, even when he didn't want to. He leaned back, grimacing as he caught sight of shattered china in a pool of tea on the table in front of him. "Well, it looks as if Hugh remedied that oversight," he muttered.

Glory felt the fight drain out of her. She had won. "Then we're through discussing this?"

Jared knew when to quit, but he had no repertoire of witty comebacks to ease the humiliation. "We're through."

"And I'll stay at Wehilani?"

"As long as you perform your job efficiently." For a moment his eyes glittered dangerously. "Or until you accuse me of prejudice again."

Glory stood, knowing an exit cue when she heard one. "I can work with a chauvinist if I have to, but working for someone who resents the descendants of the people who settled these islands would have been a waste of my time. I'm glad that's not the case."

"My people have been here for generations, too," he said, standing to face her.

"But my people *are* this island," she said quietly. "My family lived on Kauai before your family knew it existed. Our people are buried here, and their tears and laughter still linger in these mountains and valleys. Without me and those like me, Kauai would be an island without a soul." She smiled just a little, then turned and left the suite.

Jared watched her go and wondered if Wehilani would ever know peace and tranquillity again.

Chapter Two

Jared Farrell's ancestors had come to the Hawaiian Islands as missionaries and sailors. Among them they had bought up huge tracts of Kauai, the Garden Island, sometimes with nothing more than a pint of rotgut whiskey and empty promises. Jared was the last Farrell to continue to hold property on Kauai. Others had sold out long ago for astonishingly huge sums, not to the native people from whom they had wrested the land, but to hotels—and to Jared himself.

Glory Kalia's ancestors had come to the Hawaiian Islands in outrigger canoes, on ships filled to capacity with immigrants from the Philippines and Japan, and on a whaling vessel with a Boston Irish sea captain whose copper locks still gleamed merrily on the heads of some of Glory's cousins. The Kalia fortune had been measured in hard work and family love. They owned no vast estates. Only after years of struggle had Glory's mother been able to buy the tiny house where she was still raising her children.

Glory thought about the differences between herself and Jared as she made her way down to the kitchen from Jared's suite to confront Sally, the housekeeper. Hawaii was a spectacular melting pot. Within its colorful borders the most diverse people lived and worked together. She had always been happy with the diversity and proud of her state's unique heritage. She wondered if Jared Farrell, isolated on top of his own private mountain, had ever even thought about it.

The restaurant-sized Wehilani kitchen was redolent with the fragrance of roasting chicken when she entered. Glory's mother, Nola, had been the cook at the Aikane Hotel on Oahu for much of Glory's life, and Glory had learned most of her secrets. Now she judged by smell alone that the chicken was done—or overdone. If Sally was planning to serve it while it was still hot, she would have to go upstairs and yank her boss out of bed right now, prop his head up and feed it to him, bite by bite. This lapse in Sally's timing wasn't unusual. In Glory's week on the estate, she had observed meals being prepared at all hours and in all stages of disarray. She had hoped it was because the staff was alone in the big house. The roasting chicken told a different story.

Glory made her way between the stainless steel counters and the long island that dominated the work space. Sally, a tall thin woman with a sallow complexion and wispy graying hair, was bending over the oven, basting the roasting bird. Glory glimpsed chicken skin, as dark as mahogany and probably just as edible, before the oven door slammed shut.

"Sally, I want to speak to you."

Sally jumped backward, skidding on juices that had spilled as she basted. She came to a climactic stop against the counter. "You scared me to death!"

Glory was already used to Sally's dramatics. "I'm surprised you didn't hear me come in," she said politely. "Perhaps you're having a problem with your hearing today?"

Sally looked properly confused.

Glory just smiled. "Mr. Farrell tells me he called you this morning to let you know he'd be arriving today. Perhaps you didn't hear the message correctly."

Sally clapped her hand over her mouth. "Oh, no! I forgot to tell you, didn't I?"

Glory ignored the lie. "Sally, I want you to tell me what you see." Glory gestured to herself.

Sally wiped all expression from her face. "Huh?"

"What do you see?" Glory repeated, gently insistent.

"A young woman. A pretty young woman," Sally said finally.

"A young woman standing in this kitchen, at Wehilani, on the island of Kauai?"

Sally nodded.

"I stood here yesterday, didn't I?"

Sally nodded once more.

"And I'm standing here now?"

She nodded again.

"I'll be standing here tomorrow, too." Glory let her words sink in. "And the day after that," she added when it was clear that Sally understood.

Sally stopped playing games. "You weren't fired?"

"I wasn't fired."

Sally looked blank for a moment, as if the news were too much too absorb. Then she smiled, and the smile was the first genuine expression Glory had seen on her face so far that day. "I'm so glad, miss."

"And now you and I are going to have a talk about your job here and how we can organize things a little better."

Surprisingly Sally didn't blink at that bit of news, and she didn't stop smiling. She started to babble. "He didn't fire you. I can't believe it. Hugh tried to put one over on Mr. Farrell, and he's keeping you anyway. Wait'll Paradox finds out. He likes you, you know. We all do. But we knew what was going on, and we didn't think you'd stay. Boy, oh boy. This is a good one. It really is. With you looking like that Hightower woman and all."

Glory had tried hard to follow Sally's torrent of words. Now she held up her hands to cut her off. "You lost me there. Hightower woman?"

Sally nodded, now puppy-dog exuberant, her watery blue eyes snapping with life. "Patsy Hightower. Mr. Farrell's fiancée, well, she used to be, anyway. For about three months. She was Hawaiian, too, partways, you know what I mean? Like you. She had long black hair and tan skin like yours, and she was—" Sally outlined the figure eight with her hands "—curvy, like you. A real pretty lady, but none of us liked her because she wasn't making Mr. Farrell happy. And he deserves to be happy!"

"Yes. Well." Glory grabbed on to Sally's last remark to steer her back to business. "Sally, if Mr. Farrell is going to be happy, I think you'd better take the chicken out of the oven."

Sally covered her mouth like a silent-movie heroine, but she continued talking through her fingers. "I can't cook, miss. I really can't. I can clean house and keep this kitchen spotless, but I can't cook. Never learned the knack. Paradox and I trade off, but he can't cook, either. Hugh understood. We all just did the best we could after Hugh's wife died. She was the cook, you know. Mr. Farrell didn't want to hire anyone else just to cook for him. So we make do, we do."

Glory's head was beginning to spin, as if someone had sucked all the oxygen from the room. She struggled for a deep breath. "I'll give this some thought. Serious thought," she promised. "Meanwhile, get the chicken out, skin it, slice it and put it in the refrigerator. Make gravy if there's anything left to make it with. Then you can warm it up in the microwave and serve it tonight."

"Oh, no, miss. I don't use that *thing*. Radiation poison, you know." Sally raised her eyebrows spasmodically as if she had just absorbed five hundred rems and was blinking on and off like a neon sign.

"I didn't know."

"You'll learn," Sally consoled her. "And I'm sorry I didn't tell you about Mr. Farrell coming home today and all. I didn't forget. But none of us saw the sense in telling you he was coming. We thought you'd fret about meeting him, and there didn't seem to be any reason to have you fretting since nothing you could do would make him keep you on anyway."

Glory shook her head, more to clear it than anything else. "Better get the chicken."

"Glad you're here, miss."

"Glory."

Sally grinned. "Glory."

The rest of the house seemed blissfully quiet after the lively exchange in the kitchen. Glory wandered through it, making notes on a pad that was already half-full. Then she went to her office and began to type a concise room-by-room list of problems and possibilities.

She had planned to have the list ready for Mr. Farrell when he arrived on Monday. Now she wanted to present it to him tomorrow. If he agreed, she could begin to find craftsmen to repair and restore some of Wehilani's priceless antiques, hire a cook and bimonthly cleaning staff to assist Sally, and draw up a schedule so that meals were served at regular, convenient hours. It seemed like a small start, but Wehilani had been run for generations without her interference. She knew that if she didn't start slowly, no changes would be made at all.

And changes were vital. Wehilani was in no danger of collapse, but its upkeep had been slighted in the past years. The house was fifteen thousand square feet of neglect. Its rose brick exterior was overgrown by vines; its dark wood trim needed immediate protection from the elements. The outbuildings needed painting, and every roof on the property needed shingles replaced.

Then there were the gardens. She added a team of gardeners to the list. Sally's husband, Rolfe, the grounds keeper, was a ruddy potbellied man with a heavy German accent and a remarkable green thumb. But Rolfe was only one man. He could not maintain the lawn, gardens and conservatory with no help. His talents needed to be husbanded and the majority of the unskilled labor given over to others who could be brought up for a day, two or three times a month.

It was past six when Glory finished typing her report. She pushed herself away from her desk and rubbed the back of her neck. Both the weight of her hair and her responsibilities were giving her a headache. She pulled the ivory pins from her hair and let it flow down her back. The second item wasn't as easy to deal with.

She was glad to be at Wehilani, and she knew she could handle her position. What she wasn't sure she could handle was Jared Farrell.

The scene in his suite had affected her more deeply than she had revealed. She had given up her job at the Aikane Hotel and come here because living and working at Wehilani was a rare and wonderful opportunity, not only because Wehilani was a rare and wonderful place, but because once things were organized, she would have an abundance of free time to pursue her own interests.

She needed free time, and she needed Wehilani's peace and quiet if she was going to pursue the dream that had fueled every waking minute of the past five years. Now, after her meeting with Jared Farrell, she wasn't sure there would be any peace and quiet to be found.

He didn't want her here. He might have agreed to keep her on, but he would be looking over her shoulder constantly to prove that his assessment of her had been correct. Her work would be on constant display, her decisions questioned at every turn. He didn't want her, because she was young and female and resembled the woman he had almost married.

"Miss Hightower is luckier than she knows." Glory bent her head and massaged the muscles of her neck. "The man is definitely strange."

Strange, but strangely beguiling, too. Somehow just thinking about Jared Farrell with his fiancée conjured fascinating images of his long-fingered hands against warm smooth skin, blazing dark eyes lingering on feminine curves, a hard, uncompromising mouth stealing the breath from softer lips.

She was twenty-two, old enough to have played at being in love a time or two. She knew what it was like to want a man, but she had never wanted a man as badly as she had wanted her dream. She had watched her mother work and cry, then work even harder, for enough years to know that one dream at a time was all anyone was allowed. After her father's death, her mother's dream had been to raise six children to be mature, intelligent human beings. Glory's was a little different.

She wanted to translate the essence of Hawaii onto paper. She wanted to do it for children, but she wanted her pictures and her stories to be so powerful that adults loved them, too. She wanted to take Hawaii's myths and legends and breathe them to life until they flowed off the paper and into the hearts of everyone opening her books.

Wasn't that simple enough? But one complication, one detour on the road to her dreams, might render it impossible. Any man's long-fingered hands, blazing dark eyes and uncompromising mouth were more than a detour. They were a dead end.

She lifted her head and put Jared Farrell out of her mind. She would eat dinner, and then the evening would be her own. It was cool in the mountains, but there was a moonlit stream that ran through the woods about a mile behind the stables. She would bundle up and visit it tonight for inspiration. Perhaps there the voices of her ancestors would tell her how to begin to sketch her dream.

Moonlight was flooding his bedroom when Jared awoke. He had slept as only a man completely exhausted can sleep. He hadn't dreamed; he wasn't even certain he had breathed. He had just collapsed on the bed, shut his eyes and sunk into absolute oblivion.

Hunger had awakened him. Now as he sat up slowly, he realized he was ravenous. Without Glory Kalia's snack of cheese and fruit, he probably would have starved to death in his sleep.

Glory Kalia. The thought forced a growl from his throat. He had been maneuvered into a corner by Hugh, a sardonic farewell gift if ever there had been one. Jared supposed foisting Glory on him had been too irresistible for Hugh to pass up. She was everything he hadn't wanted in a manager. Now he was faced with the task of evaluating her performance like a teacher grading term papers. "A" if she saw the myriad problems around the estate and suggested improvements, "F" if she tried to use her youth and femininity as excuses not to do a competent job. "F minus" if she tried to use her youth and femininity on *him*.

Until the evaluation was completed, however, he was stuck with her. And he didn't need the headaches she would cause. He needed peace. He needed uninterrupted stretches of time so that he could think and work with no distractions. He needed the man, thirty-five or older, that he had told Hugh to hire.

Jared rose, pushing his sleep-tumbled hair off his forehead. He imagined Sally had left something for him in the kitchen. He grimaced at the thought, but he was so hungry he was even willing to eat Sally's cooking. He had traveled first-class from Athens, but he had hardly eaten a bite due to a rough flight that had stolen his appetite and his fellow passengers' calm stomachs.

Dressed and downstairs, he found a covered plate in the refrigerator. He thrust it into the microwave without viewing the contents.

Fifteen minutes later, with both sleep and food to fortify him, Jared yearned for fresh air. He had missed Wehilani. The month in Athens had been stimulating and worthwhile. He had participated in an international think tank dedicated to finding new and better ways to use the world's supply of fossil fuels. He had presented several well-received papers and come away with new ideas to contemplate. He had also come away with a yearning to be back on Kauai, where life flowed around him, not straight through him, and the air was perfumed with South Seas mystery.

Now he needed to breathe some of that air. He had a favorite place, a refuge where he often went to let the essence of Kauai soak all the way down to his soul.

He decided to ride. The path to the stream was rocky, tangled with vines and brambles, but Jared didn't want to bring a flashlight to spoil the velvet darkness. His favorite mount, a roan quarter horse named Demon, knew the way. Given his head, Demon would pick his way along the path without disturbing the evening stillness.

In the stables, he saddled Demon himself. One Leg—an Australian who had picked up the nickname as a young man when he had triumphed in an outback race with one leg in a cast—was gone for the evening, camping, as he so loved to do, in the far reaches of the Na Pali coast. Demon nuzzled Jared's hand, hoping for and finding a piece of apple.

Up on the horse, Jared felt the peace of evening begin to steal over him. He guided Demon around the stables and through a rock-lined entrance to the path.

The night was the definition of darkness. The horse and rider immersed themselves in the midst of it until they had become one with the black rain-saturated clouds that veiled the moon.

There was no moonlight to etch silver webs of light on the rocks that lined the forest stream. Glory had never been so completely surrounded by darkness. There had been moonlight on the path, but as she had neared the stream, it had been swallowed by the clouds, imprisoning her so that each step she took was an act of faith.

She wasn't afraid. There were no predators except possibly wild boar to concern herself with. The path was overgrown, but the forest that flanked it was so dense that she had little chance of wandering into it. And she could hear the musical flow of water over rocks, rushing toward the waterfall downstream that formed a shallow, perfect pool for swimming.

She had never made it as far as the falls. The way was difficult, narrow and rocky. She planned to go there one day when she had a whole morning free, preferably a warm morning when she could swim in the icy pool as her ancestors must once have done.

Now, though, she concentrated on just finding the stream. The rush of water grew louder as she moved through the forest until she thought she saw the dim outline of the rocks where she had hoped to find ideas for her sketches.

Tonight she would find no scenes for sketching, but that wouldn't stop her from dreaming and listening. She would wait at the rocks, absorbing the very essence of a Hawaiian night. Then, if she was lucky, the moon would defeat the clouds once more, and she could easily find her way back.

Once she had reached the rocks, she settled in a comfortable spot where she could lean back and listen to the soft musical song of the water.

So many stories of the Hawaiian people were myths of water and moonlight, of fire's glow and the deepest dark of night. She listened, and she imagined what it must have been like to have lived here in a village in the mountains, generations before missionaries or sailors had come bringing a different culture to change the islands forever.

The ride to the stream seemed too short. Jared realized how much he had missed the deep Wehilani stillness. The silence was broken only by the buzz of insects and the occasional chorus of a night bird. As he rode closer to the stream, however, he could hear its tireless melody.

"We're almost there," he told Demon, leaning forward to pat the horse's neck.

Demon whinnied as if in response.

Jared's laugh was deep and unfettered, the sound of a man who feels as if he's been released from civilization's chains. Demon whinnied again, then once more.

Jared's laughter ceased abruptly. Demon sensed something or someone, and he was showing his concern. He was a high-strung, intelligent animal who, more than once in the past, had alerted Jared to trouble.

Jared peered through the darkness, reining Demon to a halt. The horse danced with impatience beneath him, but Jared held him steady. "Who's there?" he called.

The night was so black that he could barely make out a thin silhouette rising from the rocks beside the stream.

"Glory."

For a moment Jared refused to accept the obvious. This spot was his. To his knowledge none of the staff ever trespassed here, although there was no rule forbidding them. As he rode closer he wondered if he had conjured her presence. Surrounded by night she looked like a forest wraith, a breathtakingly beautiful ghost of Hawaii's past.

But ghosts didn't wear sweaters and jeans. Jared dismounted, then dropped Demon's reins to the ground. The horse had once been used for cattle roundups on a ranch near Lihue and knew the signal. Now he stood without moving as Jared walked toward Glory.

Even the ordinary clothes she wore couldn't hide Glory's exotic beauty. The sparkling white of the cowl-necked sweater was a beautiful contrast to the creamy hue of her skin and the black of her hair, which spilled over the back of the sweater like a dark waterfall. The jeans molded the graceful curve of her hips and the sleek length of her legs. But even as one part of him admired her, another questioned.

"What are you doing here?"

She wondered whether being forbidden to visit the stream was one more thing the rest of the staff had conveniently forgotten to tell her. "I was just enjoying the silence. I'm sorry. Would you prefer I didn't come here?"

It was clear that if he said yes, she wouldn't come again, and she wouldn't ask why. "Wehilani is yours to enjoy while you're here," Jared said. "Nothing is off-limits. But you shouldn't be here on a night like this one." He scowled up at the clouds partially veiling the moon. "It's probably going to rain any time now."

"The sky was clear when I left the house. But I'm not afraid of rain."

"This isn't a warm tropical rain, Miss Kalia. You're in the mountains, now. It will chill you to the bone."

He saw the gleam of white teeth as his answer. She wasn't going to argue, but she put no stock in his warning. He grew more irritated. "I'm surprised you found your way in the dark. You must have had a powerful flashlight."

"No flashlight." She held up her hands to show they were empty. "The moon guided me partway, the stream the rest. I've been here several times this week, so I knew the path."

"And if you'd wandered off it by mistake, you might have gotten lost."

"I would have survived the night. Others have." She turned back toward the stream, seating herself on a rock. "I was thinking about Koolau when I heard your horse...." Her voice trailed off as if she were thinking of him again.

Despite himself, Jared was intrigued. He knew the story, but he waited, wondering if she would tell it.

"He was a leper," she said softly as if she were speaking to herself. "But when they came to take him to Molokai to abandon him to the elements and early death, he hid in these mountains. He didn't want to leave his family, so he hid, and armies of men couldn't find him. His wife must have loved him very much, because she escaped into the mountains, too, whenever she could, to bring him food and comfort. Then, one day, she found nothing but his bones. She buried them in the mountains at the place where he had died and never told anyone the location."

Jared heard the emotion in the soft lilt of her words. He knew that for the seconds it had taken her to tell the legend, she had lived it. He was strangely touched for a moment, transported by the power of the simple love story. Then he thought about what it meant.

He hardened his heart. "It's nothing more than a story told to tourists."

"No, it really happened."

"Oh, there was a leper named Koolau, certainly, who escaped into the mountains. But the rest is sentiment."

Glory smiled, and the smile sounded in her voice. "You were there, then?"

Jared moved to a rock behind her and leaned against it, folding his arms. "Have you ever met a woman that dedicated to a man? Koolau's wife probably ran screaming into the night when she found he had leprosy. If she buried his bones, it was to stop the spread of the disease."

"I've met several women that dedicated to their men. Our mutual friend Toby Chandler is one of them."

Jared was surprised. "You know Toby?"

"You haven't looked at my résumé, have you? I learned everything I know about hotel management from her. She and Cole are my dearest friends."

He let this new piece of information sink in. "Is that how you found out about the job here?"

"Toby spoke to Hugh before I even knew about it. She arranged my interview."

"No wonder he hired a woman. After Hugh spoke to Toby, he was probably so confused, he couldn't remember what he was supposed to do."

Glory felt no insult. Toby did have that effect on people. It was part of her charm. But Glory had to point out the obvious, too. "Hugh hired me because I was well qualified, and undoubtedly because I looked like Patsy Hightower."

"Another mutual friend?" he asked coldly.

"No. Sally told me about her today."

"You'll find we have few secrets from each other at Wehilani, but I don't appreciate idle gossip."

"It's not idle when it concerns my employment here." Glory turned so that she was facing Jared. "I want to stay, but I also want you to know I'm not Patsy Hightower. I'm me. Please don't expect trouble just because I'm an island woman with long dark hair and—" she copied Sally's figure eight with her hands "—curves."

Jared didn't want to smile. He didn't want to like Glory Kalia. But the night was just light enough that he could see the mischief in her eyes. His lips tilted skyward on their own.

The first drops of rain christened them both simultaneously. Jared stood. "It's time to get back." He had smiled at Glory, but he wanted no further intimacies. He couldn't leave her here, though, to make her way through the forest on a slick, dark path. "Do you know how to ride, Miss Kalia?"

"Quite well, Mr. Farrell."

Raindrops bounced off Jared's thick brown hair to run down his nose. He watched in fascination as water droplets beaded like black diamonds on Glory's hair and sparkled against her skin. He was smiling again before either of them knew why.

"I only have one horse... Glory."

"He looks strong enough for two... Jared."

He nodded as if something more important than her equestrian skills had been decided. Then he turned and made his way up the path to the place where a restless Demon was standing. He grasped the reins and mounted, then waited until Glory joined him and bent to give her a hand up. He pulled, and she leaped with the dancer grace he already associated with her. She settled in front of him as if they had ridden together this way forever. She leaned back, and he circled her with his arms. Her hair was a silken cape between them, and he inhaled the clean fragrance that seemed a part of her.

Demon rocked gently beneath them as they started up the path. Jared hadn't known he was cold until the heat of Glory's body, nestled against his in the confines of the saddle, began to warm him. More than her warmth was a surprise. She was too soft to be so slender, and yet the truth was undeniable. Her body bounced gently against his, and he could feel each cuddly inch. It was a body to give a man sleepless nights.

They had been at Wehilani together for only hours, and already he was holding her in his arms. He stiffened, but there was no room to withdraw. Her sweater rubbed against his chest; her hair tickled his chin. Her very essential femininity stirred his blood.

They were almost to the stables before Glory spoke. She had been strangely moved by the ride and by the strong arms of the man behind her. "Koolau's wife loved him," she said as if they hadn't spoken of anything else. "She stood by him until he died. And he loved her enough to fight to stay with her. Why would you want to believe otherwise?"

"The difference between a realist and a dreamer."

Perhaps it was the return of the moonlight after what had only been a light rain. Perhaps it was the magic of a Kauai night. Whatever it was, Glory ignored the fact that the man who held her so securely was a stranger and her reluctant employer. "You've been hurt," she said sadly. "But that's only a part of reality, Jared. The other part is dreams."

He didn't answer as he guided Demon into the stables, where he watched Glory slide to the straw-covered floor.

"Good night." She smiled up at him, her face still beaded with raindrops.

He nodded curtly. The night had touched him, too. Worse, the woman had thawed something in him that would have better remained frozen. "If you decide to visit the stream at night, take a light or a horse. But don't go unprepared again. I might not be there to rescue you next time."

"Did I thank you?" she asked.

"There's no need. It was a simple thing I would have done for anyone."

"But it's the simple things that make us human, isn't it?" She was still smiling. "Thank you, anyway." She turned and left the stables. She didn't know that his eyes followed her, or that he sat there for a long time after she had gone, wondering if the brief warmth they had shared had been a simple thing at all.

Chapter Three

Glory was sitting alone in the kitchen with a cup of steaming coffee and a book when Jared walked through the door the next morning. She was so absorbed in what she was reading that he had a moment to study her before she looked up and realized he was there.

Today she was obviously dressed for her role as estate manager, although by Jared's calculations it was Sunday and, in the spirit of the missionary family who had established Wehilani, no one should be working. He took in the intricate braids that drew her hair back from her face and ended in a woven knot at her nape, the suit of a sensible gray-and-black stripe, the gray print blouse. She was a wondrous bird of paradise disguised in the feathers of a sparrow. For just a moment he longed to see her with none of the trappings of civilization. Ignoring orders not to, his mind formed a vision of Glory, naked, her hair streaming down her back, on a deserted Kauai beach.

"Good morning, Jared." Glory smiled up at the man who was frowning as if the morning wasn't good at all. He was dressed casually in a dark green polo shirt and gray pants.

His hair, which was slightly too long, as if he couldn't be bothered with something as mundane as a haircut, fell over his forehead, accentuating, not detracting from, his aristocratic good looks.

"I just made coffee," she continued, trying not to notice how appealing he was this way, half-asleep and cranky. "Would you like some? Sally tells me you don't eat breakfast."

"I'll get it."

"There's coconut macadamia coffee cake, too."

Jared's body was not complying with the simplest directions. His mouth watered at the mention of the cake. He knew better. "I never eat in the mornings," he grumbled. "Sally's cooking is hard enough to take when I'm fully awake."

Glory nodded sympathetically. "I know. So I made the coffee cake. The Aikane's famous for it. It's my mother's recipe."

Once Jared had visited Toby and Cole Chandler at their villa on the windward coast of Oahu, and Toby had taken him to see the Aikane hotel, which she managed in trust for her half brother and half sister, who were still children. For a moment he stepped back in time and remembered....

"I've had it before," he said slowly. "When I was visiting the hotel with Toby. And I would have met your mother, but she was away for the evening because she was giving a party."

Glory was surprised. "When was that?"

"A year ago, or a little more. June, I think. Toward the end of the month."

"My birthday party," Glory said. "My twenty-first. It was a family event. Every relative well or old enough to crawl came to celebrate. I'm surprised Toby didn't drag you there." She paused, recreating the night for herself. "But she couldn't have, could she?" she asked as memories formed, "because she went into labor."

"She was *in* labor as she was showing me the hotel. Cole just got her into Honolulu in time."

Glory was grinning. "I've heard the story a dozen times. Toby thought she had an annoying backache. It never occurred to her that she was in labor, because—"

Jared didn't miss a beat. "Because labor means working hard, and Toby insisted there was nothing she could do about a backache, much less work hard."

"In all fairness to Toby," Glory reminded him, "Nicky was a little early."

"Toby took ten years off my life. We were walking out through the hotel gardens, and she stopped suddenly. She rested her hands on her belly and said, 'You might want to call Cole, Jared, dear. I may be having his baby any minute.'"

Glory laughed. Jared's imitation of Toby's blithe tone in the face of disaster was perfect. "And Nicky was born on my birthday. All six pounds of him."

Jared smiled a little. "Last time I saw him, he was twenty pounds of gorgeous."

Glory watched Jared fill his coffee cup, then take a slice of cake. Her smile died as she realized that they were chatting in the kitchen like two old friends. Only they weren't old friends; Jared was her employer. For a moment she didn't know what to do. Would he want the kitchen to himself? Would he take his plate and cup into the mammoth formal dining room for more distance? Wehilani was certainly large enough for everyone, but at a time like this, it seemed surprisingly small.

Jared had no qualms about what to do. He sat down across from Glory and started on his coffee cake. "What are you reading?"

Her eyes dropped to the book in front of her. "It's a collection of stories about Hawaii."

"What kind?"

"Legends about heroes." She looked up and saw that he seemed interested. "The hero or *kupua* is a recurring theme in our folklore. He's always a man of extraordinary powers, but he uses his powers for the sake of others, not for his personal gain."

"And why does that interest you?"

She didn't want to tell Jared about her dream. It was a private one, shared with only the most important people in her life. She would not subject it to Jared's scrutiny. "Aren't all women interested in heroes?"

"In my experience, women are more interested in men with lots of money."

Glory wished he would say more, but she knew it wasn't her place to ask. "Then you'd probably enjoy reading about a culture where money as we know it didn't exist."

Jared was surprised that Glory would be interested in mythology. He tried to imagine Patsy reading anything more profound than *Cosmopolitan*. For that matter, it wasn't only Patsy. He had met warm, intelligent women in his life, but all of them had been either married or over sixty. The women who relentlessly threw themselves at him were either practicing airheads or so dedicated to securing his wealth that they had no time to indulge their intellects.

Of course, there was no question that some of his problems with women had been his own fault. He was a recluse, a hermit, and he lived in his imagination, with only his thoughts as companions. He could relate to people if he was forced to, and he was a good judge of character if he took the time to make the judgment. But far too often he had neither the time nor the interest. He preferred his solitude to endless male-female games, the culling of the fortune hunters, the encouragement of those with real potential.

Until Patsy. Perhaps he'd been a fool because he was approaching thirty when he met her. Perhaps it was because he had just begun to see what his life was missing, influenced by friends like Toby and Cole and their fine family. He had believed he was falling in love with Patsy, and he had begun to have fantasies of a family of his own. He had even asked her to be his wife. Then he had discovered just who and what she was.

"I'll loan you the book when I'm finished," Glory said, setting her coffee cup on the table. "You might find it interesting."

Glory's offer successfully pulled Jared out of his thoughts, but he was left with a familiar residue of bitterness. And a resolve. He wasn't going to let another woman into his life. He didn't have time or energy for love. He didn't even have time for friendship.

"Don't bother." He stood, pushing his chair behind him with a loud scrape. "I've got a stack of journals a mile high in my lab. That's where I'll be today."

Glory wondered what had changed Jared's mood so radically. He had gone from grumpy to pleasant to frozen. The room had a distinct chill, and she had the feeling she should address her next question to "Mr. Farrell" or perhaps "my lord."

Out of principle, she did neither. She smiled pleasantly, as if he hadn't been rude. "Jared, will you have some time to meet with me today? I've typed up a list that I'd like to go over with you."

"What kind of list?" His eyes darkened with suspicion.

For a moment she wished she had just waited for a better time. But the man was so volatile that there was probably no way to gauge just the right second to sandwich in her request. As she answered, she prepared herself for rejection. "Some possible changes."

"You've been here just a week."

Although the rest of his sentence was unspoken, she heard it clearly. What could she possibly have learned in such a short time?

"A week was long enough to see a number of the more serious problems," she said calmly. "A day would have been long enough for some of them. I'll admit the subtleties might take longer, but we'd want to correct the most important problems first, anyway."

Jared wasn't normally an irritable man. Nor was he an irrational one. He had sanctioned the hiring of an estate manager, and even if a trick had been played on him, Glory Kalia was now his employee. She was just doing the job she was being paid to do. He knew his own reaction was way out of bounds, but for the moment, he had no control over it.

"I don't want to discuss anything today," he said sharply. "I'm sure you've been told we don't work on Sundays at Wehilani. Everyone deserves a day of rest."

Her eyes didn't waver, nor did they show that his reprimand had hurt her. "I'm sorry. Unfortunately, no one's told me the ground rules."

He sighed in exasperation. When had he become such a tyrant? Glory's eyes were still searching his calmly, as if she could read his turmoil and wanted to know how to respond. "No, I'm the one who should be sorry," he said at last. "I didn't mean to bite your head off. Maybe I'd better take my own advice and take the day off, too. Apparently I need the rest."

Her lips curved into a smile. She could see his apology had been genuine. "It's a beautiful day. The sun is actually shining. I'm sure Demon would like a day out of the stables."

He wasn't sure what motivated his next question, but it was out of his mouth before he'd had time to think. "How much of the estate have you seen?"

"The immediate grounds and the path to the stream."

"If you're going to manage Wehilani, you've got to see it."

"I've been waiting for your permission to use one of the horses."

"Surely someone told you that goes with your position?"

She shook her head. "I'm afraid no one thought I'd stay once you met me. I imagine they didn't think it was wise to tell me anything."

He admired her good humor. In her place he would have been furious. "Have you noticed the gray mare beside Demon in the stable?"

"Ghost? She's a beauty."

"She'll be yours while you're here." He hesitated, then committed himself to the plan that had been forming. "Why not try her out today? I'll show you some of Wehilani." He smiled reluctantly. "Bring your list."

* * *

Moody, difficult to get along with, autocratic. Jared listed the qualities that seemed to characterize him these days. He wanted to lay the blame for his inconsistencies at Patsy's doorstep, but Patsy had never been that important to him. The idea of what she could bring to his life had been more important. He had wanted to love her, but he had loved the idea of love more.

Demon danced impatiently as Jared tightened the saddle's girth. One Leg made sure that each horse got regular exercise, but Demon was used to long, exhausting rides through the mountains with Jared on his back. Jared could sense he was looking forward to this day. He led the prancing quarter horse out of the stall and dropped his reins by the doorway. Then he went to the next stall to begin saddling Ghost.

"I could have done that." Glory came into the immaculately kept stables and stood in the doorway, stroking Demon's muzzle as her eyes adjusted to the dimmer light.

"I'll show you which tack to use so you'll know next time."

Glory went to the door of the stall and watched Jared with Ghost. "She's really a beauty. Have you bred her?"

"We may in the future."

"Then you'll have a little ghostling."

"Banshee."

"Why all the scary names?"

Jared turned to look at her. She had changed into jeans and a bright blue aloha shirt. Her hair was still braided, but now the braids spilled down her back. "When I was a boy and we visited here, my parents wanted me to be good. So they'd warn me about the ghosts and demons in the stables that were just waiting to grab little boys."

Glory's answering smile faded.

Jared turned back to the mare. "Not good child psychology, I suppose. My father was a product of parents who had done the same. The past fades slowly sometimes. When Wehilani became mine and I decided to fill the stables, I named the horses after all those childhood fears." Even as he was telling Glory the story, he wondered why.

"At least your children can see that the ghosts and demons here are nothing to fear." Glory opened the stall door and held Ghost's bridle as Jared threw on the saddle blanket, then the saddle.

Jared watched Glory stroke the mare's muzzle. "Where did you learn to ride?"

"All my sisters and I are *pau* riders. We've ridden in parades since we were old enough to stand, not in the fancier parades, but in smaller ones."

"*Pau* riders?"

"You're not a parade goer, I take it." She quickly summed up the old tradition. "When the first horses arrived in the islands as gifts to King Kamehameha, the island girls wanted to ride astride. Of course the sailors who had brought the horses were appalled. So they showed them how to make riding costumes with wide legs and shawls. As the years went by, the costumes were adapted to reflect the color of the islands. We wear long split skirts and long puff-sleeved blouses. In the more traditional clubs, yards and yards of fabric are draped over riding clothes, then pinned in place, so the rider looks like an island goddess once she's mounted. But in our club, we've adapted a simpler version. We garland the horses with leis we make ourselves. It's quite a spectacle."

"And can you really ride that way?"

"Like the wind."

He tightened Ghost's girth. "How many sisters do you have?"

"Two. I've got three brothers, too. Two of them are married, but the little one, Jeff, is only fourteen. The same age as Skates."

Jared knew that Skates was Toby Chandler's half brother. Toby's father had been a bigamist. A salesman, he had been married to Toby's mother in Kansas, but he had also been secretly married to an island woman. When he had died in an accident, and his Hawaiian wife had died with him, Toby had discovered that she had a brother and sister. With her usual compassion and total disregard for possible problems, she had come to Hawaii to assume the care of the two children. "You're not by any chance related to—"

"Skates and Lani?" Glory nodded. "They're my cousins. Their mother was my mother's sister." She watched Jared try to make sense of the complicated relationship. "So I'm not related to Toby, but I am related to her brother and sister. Of course, I grew up calling her father 'Uncle,' so—"

"You can stop now."

She laughed. "None of that matters, anyway. Toby is family. She just is. And now so are Cole and little Nicky."

He felt a surprising twinge of envy at the love with which the words had been spoken. It was clear that Glory was part of a large, happy network of people who, whether they were blood relatives or not, mattered greatly to each other. "It's going to be very lonely up here."

"Maybe. I prefer to think it's just going to be very quiet." She wondered if he would understand her next words. "I've longed for quiet most of my life."

Jared looked up and caught a surprisingly wistful look on Glory's face. Her serenity was like a blanket that usually smothered any traces of her other emotions. Now he knew he was catching a glimpse of a different young woman.

She smiled, and the expression was gone. "I can hardly wait to try this little beauty." She turned and led Ghost out of the stall, keeping her well away from Demon's heels. Jared brushed past her and mounted. Turning his head, he saw that Glory had mounted, too.

"I thought we'd ride along the borders today, just to give you a sense of how large Wehilani really is."

"I've seen it all from the helicopter, but everything's dwarfed that way."

Jared nodded, then guided Demon out of the stables. Glory followed behind.

* * *

They rode for an hour without stopping. Jared had expected a barrage of questions, but Glory was silent most of the way, seeming to enjoy nothing more than the sounds of the horses' shoes ringing against stones on the narrow path. She controlled Ghost with little effort, and after only minutes of watching her progress, Jared knew he could trust her with any horse in the stables. Glory was small, but she was strong and confident enough to show the mare who was in charge.

Wehilani unfolded before them like a tourist brochure. The land was a piece of old Hawaii. Never touched by the hands of developers, streams never harnessed for energy, forest never harvested for lumber, Wehilani was a superbly kept secret. If it hadn't been for the tourists circling overhead in helicopters, Glory would have been able to pretend she and Jared were alone on the island—on the earth, perhaps—Adam and Eve in a Garden of Eden that surely must be as exquisite as the original.

"Hawaii's state bird," Jared said, grimacing toward the sky as yet another helicopter passed overhead.

"I've got a good idea for you," she said, laughing at his expression. "Invent a silent helicopter."

"Silent *and* invisible."

"I know how the people flying overhead feel, though, don't you? Most of them have such a little bit of time to get to know the islands. A day here, two days there. They want to see it all. Paradise in eight days and seven nights. Then memories for a lifetime."

"Sympathy for tourists? I'm surprised."

"We're all tourists if we leave our homeland. I went to Kansas once, with Toby. I gawked at everything, bought silly souvenirs. Toby told me I was the only real tourist her little town had ever seen. She predicted the local chamber of commerce was going to throw me a banquet."

"Or put you in an asylum."

They rode a little farther until they came to a small peaceful valley between two tall peaks. "State land," Jared said, motioning beyond them.

Because of the mountains, Glory couldn't see it, but she knew that the ocean lay miles beyond Wehilani's boundaries. In between, to the west, was the rugged Na Pali coastline. Wehilani was a gentler place, its terrain difficult but not impassable. Beyond, the forest was so dense and wild that there were rumored to be dozens of undetected homesteaders surviving off the land. Some farmed, as it were, although their crops were neither legal nor wholesome.

"Are you ready to stop?" Jared asked.

"Any time you are." Glory followed Jared to a grove of koa trees and dismounted. There was a shallow brook that wound its way through rocks at the edge of the grove, and, following Jared's lead, she led Ghost there to drink.

"You can drop her reins. She'll stay close by." Jared took a knapsack off Demon's saddle and a rolled blanket. "Let's find a place to have our sandwiches."

It was still early, but Glory realized she was hungry, too. She helped Jared spread the blanket under the shade of a large tree, then sat down beside him to help spread out their lunch. "Can we eat all this?" she asked, surprised at the bounty. There were chicken sandwiches, mangoes, a small wheel of Gouda cheese and rich squares of baklava that he had obviously brought home from his trip to Greece.

"I can eat it all," he assured her. "So dig in if you don't want me to."

Glory didn't need any more warning than that. She was almost through her chicken sandwich and half her cheese before she spoke again. "This is the best meal I've had since I arrived."

"Except for breakfast."

"All the stars in the heavens must be aligned just right today. I wonder what we'll have for dinner."

Jared was uncomfortably aware of how close Glory was sitting. She had little choice; the blanket was small and square. But she'd seemed too close as she'd ridden beside him, too. She had an allure that was difficult to ignore no matter how far away she was. She was certainly not the middle-aged man who would have left Jared's life focused on his work.

He shoved away his thoughts. "Is that a cue to discuss your list?"

"We don't have to. I'll be happy to wait until it's convenient." She risked a smile. "And I don't want to spoil a beautiful day."

Jared leaned back and propped his head on a hand, stretching his legs in front of him. His face was farther from Glory now, but his long legs brushed her jeans. "Let's hear it."

For a moment she felt tongue-tied. Jared Farrell was her boss, and only just that. She had known him for less than twenty-four hours; his moods were lightning quick and his opinion of women in general as low as a snake. But if all those things were true, why did she have a curious feeling deep inside her just because his legs were resting against hers?

She breathed deeply, trying to ease tension she didn't want to understand. "Shall we start with the house or the grounds?"

"Whichever you prefer."

"The house, then." She pulled the list from the back pocket of her jeans. "Before we talk about staff problems, I've made a list of furniture that needs repair or refinishing. There are a few pieces I'm really worried about, because without work, I'm afraid they're going to be beyond repair in a short time. There's the—"

"Have an expert come up and examine the lot. I don't care. If an expert agrees, I'm perfectly amenable to having things refinished, repaired or thrown on the trash heap."

"Trash heap?" Glory looked up from her list, astounded. "We're talking about priceless antiques, aren't we? That table in the dining room must be worth a fortune, and it's on its last legs."

"Its first legs. My great-great-grandfather had it shipped from his ancestral home in Wales in the mid-eighteen hundreds. It was probably old then."

"Yes, well." She couldn't think of one comment to make that wasn't judgmental. If Jared had no sense of the value, both historical and monetary, of the table, she wasn't the one to educate him. "I'll call several experts and get their opinions. Then I'll tell you what they find."

He shrugged.

Glory continued. "The inside of the house seems in fairly good repair, although there are two spare bedrooms that need painting, and the floor in the lady's parlor could use refinishing."

"Paradox likes to paint. A professional should do the floor."

"And I have your permission to take care of that?"

"You do." Jared shifted just a little. His leg now rested more firmly against Glory's, but the cramp that had twinged along his calf from the tension of avoiding her was eased. "Go on."

"That brings us to staff." She plunged right in, ignoring the warmth spreading up her leg. "There's a real staff shortage, Jared. I think most of the problems can be handled without hiring live-ins, except for one position, and that's a cook. I know all of you have gotten used to catching meals when you can and eating what either Paradox or Sally puts together, but the fact is that the food at Wehilani's appalling. You shouldn't have to put up with it. You deserve three well-prepared meals a day, and when you entertain, you need food that's fit to serve your guests."

Jared reminded himself that he was paying Glory to manage Wehilani. He had no reason to feel grateful that she was thinking of his needs. Still, warmth crept into his voice. "I do?"

"You do," she said, nodding her conviction. "I don't know how you've managed this long without one."

"It won't be easy to find a cook who's willing to come up here, away from everything and everyone."

"I'll find you someone, and I'll do it right away. What kind of food do you prefer?"

He pretended to give the matter serious thought. "French? Continental? Japanese?" He snapped his fingers. "Rare food."

Glory frowned. "Like peacock tongues? Greens from the top of a living volcano."

"Rare food. Food that Sally hasn't burned."

She laughed, appreciating the sparkle in his brown eyes. "Then I take it you're not a picky man."

"Find me someone who'll take less than half an hour to cook a three-minute egg and I'll be her slave."

She wondered why he hadn't hired someone himself or had Hugh do it. But the answer was easy to guess. Jared didn't want to think about Wehilani. He was a man who rarely thought about his own comfort or his surroundings. She was suddenly glad she was there to do his thinking for him.

"If Sally doesn't cook, she'll be able to do what she likes best, and that's clean. But she'll still need help." Glory outlined her plan to bring in staff on a bimonthly basis. Then she progressed to the outside of the building and the grounds and her thoughts on helping Rolfe. Jared nodded his acceptance of each item. Finally she folded her list. "That's it for now."

Jared saw the satisfaction on her face. He knew that even if she hadn't admitted it to herself, she had wanted to prove something. For a moment she seemed impossibly young and innocent. He wanted to tell her not to let anyone's opinion of her matter that much; then he realized that he wanted his opinion to matter. And he wasn't sure why.

"You've done a good job," he said. "I've known about all those problems, but I just haven't wanted to face them."

"Well, that's why you hired me." She laughed a little. "I mean, that's why Hugh hired me."

Jared reached over and touched her arm lightly. Her skin was soft and smooth, and his fingertips asked to linger. He didn't let them. "Glory Kalia," he said, holding her gaze as he lifted his hand, "may I hire you to manage my estate?"

"Yes. I'd like that."

Glory's eyes were shining happily, and there was a faint blush on her cheeks. Jared didn't want the moment to end. But he knew that moments became minutes, and minutes days and weeks. He knew well how days and weeks destroyed everything between a man and a woman. He drew his legs up and stood. "Let's save the baklava for later, shall we? If we're going to see even half the border land today, we should get going."

Glory stood, too, watching Jared's long stride as he went for the horses. For a moment she forgot that he was her employer. He was only a man, and despite a well-developed sense of what was right and sensible, she wondered what it would be like to really know the Jared Farrell who had just hired her for the job she already held.

They mounted and rode for another hour before they turned back toward the house, choosing a different path than the one that had taken them this far. They rode in silence, progressing single file through a narrow gorge when Jared reined Demon to a sharp halt. Glory had to work to control Ghost, who reared at the sudden change in plans.

"What is it?" she called.

Jared didn't answer for a moment; then he turned. "Trespassers."

She wasn't afraid. Instead she felt sorry for the people who could inspire that much anger in Jared's eyes.

"Stay here. I'm going to have a few words with them." Jared nudged Demon, and the quarter horse continued through the gorge.

Glory had no intention of disobeying Jared's orders, but she pulled up close enough to see what was happening. Fifty yards into the peaceful valley beyond the gorge were two backpackers' tents. Four packs leaned against the stump of a freshly hacked tree. The tree itself lay in crudely chopped chunks around a camp fire as makeshift seats for two long-haired men and a short-haired woman.

The tree wasn't the only visible sign of the backpackers' disregard for the land they were camping on. A third man in swim trunks was bathing in the small creek that meandered past their campsite. Glory could see the suds from his shampoo washing across the rocks and logs downstream.

"You're on private property." Jared sat on his horse above the campers like a prince on his throne.

The backpackers, with the exception of one young man, looked like properly chastened subjects.

"Hey, man!" The obviously unrepentant man stood. "We're not hurting anything. It's not like we plan to live here forever or anything. We're just soaking up the atmosphere, you know?"

"How would you like to soak up the atmosphere in the Lihue jail?" Jared asked.

The lone woman stood, too, obviously frightened. "We can be out of here in twenty minutes."

The man who was standing turned to her. "He can't do anything. There aren't any police in the middle of nowhere."

Jared pointed toward the sky. "On Kauai, the police can come from any direction."

"We'd better go," the woman said.

The man didn't listen. "We're just here visiting. From Chicago. You've got no right to throw us out. Maybe you've got some fancy piece of paper that says you own this place, but—"

"Friend," Jared said, his voice dangerously calm, "I've got more than a piece of paper. I have a feeling for this land that you obviously don't. Now you take your tents and your backpacks and you get going. After you've gone, I'll see what I can do to erase the fact that you were ever here."

There was grumbling, but it was obvious that he had finally reached them all. Jared rode back to where Glory waited and stayed beside her. When the backpackers were ready to leave, he pointed in the direction he and Glory had come from. "There's state land about three hours that way and a clearly marked path once you're on it. I own a chopper. My pilot will be patrolling this area just before nightfall. He flew in Nam, so he'll know where to look for you."

Jared waited until the backpackers were gone before he spoke again. He turned to Glory as if asking her to understand, but his words were enigmatic. "Wehilani is mine. Sometimes, like now, I think she's more a burden than a blessing."

"Would it have hurt to let them stay? I know they weren't treating the land with respect, but maybe if you'd talked to them about not cutting down any more trees..."

Jared was already shaking his head. "And then I'd have to talk to the next group and the next. No, Wehilani is mine, and I protect what's mine the way I protect my privacy. I can't allow trespassers here." He dismounted and walked toward the camp fire to be sure the backpackers had smothered it. Glory followed and began to roll the logs toward a grove of trees.

In a short time it was as if the small valley had never been inhabited.

Chapter Four

Glory knew that Jared's personal hiring of her was only the first step in her acceptance as Wehilani's manager. He was giving her a chance to prove herself, and she spent the next weeks working hard to do just that.

Her first order of business was to call the staff together to outline the changes she was going to make. She had expected any number of reactions, but the one she got—total cooperation—was a pleasant surprise.

The guarantee of a cook was met with joy. Glory ran an ad in both *The Garden Island*, Kauai's newspaper, and the two Honolulu papers. The responses were slow in coming, but by the end of the two weeks, she had answered one that seemed promising. She made several trips by helicopter to Lihue, the largest town on the island, for interviews for house and grounds staff and for choosing a company to assess the repairs on the estate's antiques. After a flurry of activity, she was left with only the decision about a cook.

It was with a certain amount of trepidation that, three weeks after the ride along Wehilani's borders, Glory bearded the lion in his den—or, more accurately, the hermit in his cave. She had seen little of Jared in the intervening weeks. She had set definite times for meals, supervising and helping with their preparation, but Jared had requested that his meals be brought to his suite, so she hadn't even caught a glimpse of him then.

Apparently his request wasn't unusual. Paradox explained that when Jared was thinking, he wanted no disturbances. The estate was to function normally, as if he weren't there. Even if Jared was seen walking through the vast hallways or on the grounds, the staff only nodded politely, so as not to destroy his train of thought.

Strangely, the polite distance between employer and staff had no overtones of master-servant. When addressing him, all the staff called Jared by his first name. They fussed over his welfare as if he were a favored son, and from all accounts, they scolded him if he didn't take care of himself to their satisfaction. Jared, in turn, treated them with affection that held no condescension. He truly was the man who had allowed his estate to fall into disrepair rather than retire Hugh.

But he was also a man who could isolate himself so thoroughly that he might as well be alone on the planet.

It was that man Glory hated to approach. She stood outside his door, holding his breakfast tray, on a morning when thin slivers of sunlight dotted the Wehilani landscape and raised her hand to knock.

"Just leave the tray, Sally. I'll heat it up later," Jared called through the closed door.

"It's not Sally," Glory called back. "I need to talk to you, Jared. May I see you for a moment?"

There was no answer. Then the door was flung open. The man standing in the doorway was fresh from the shower, hair still dripping. He wore a white terry-cloth robe belted over a body that was still beaded with moisture. Glory's gaze fastened on the tiny droplets caught in the dark hair visible on his chest. She forced her eyes up to the scowl on his face.

"I know I'm bothering you," she began.

"Let's not have our conversation out here." He turned and started through the suite, stooping to retrieve a towel he had dropped on the floor. He rubbed his hair as he walked.

Glory set the tray in his kitchen, then followed him into the living room. Jared was already sprawled on the sofa, and he gestured to the chair beside him.

"I'll make this quick," she promised.

He waved his hand as if to erase her words. "You're not disturbing me." He almost laughed as soon as the words were out of his mouth. It was the biggest lie he'd ever uttered. Of course she was disturbing him. She had disturbed him since the first moment he'd seen her standing in her office. Errant thoughts of her had disturbed his concentration as he'd tried to sketch out the plans for an improvement on the gadget that was saving precious gasoline and making him a millionaire many times over. She had disturbed every masculine part of him since he had touched her skin and felt its resilience, leaned his leg against hers and felt her warmth.

She had disturbed him, and what disturbed him most was that he had let her.

Glory smiled at what seemed like encouragement. "That's good. Then you're coming up for air?"

"I'm taking a break, if that's what you mean."

"Then my timing's good. I need your opinion about a cook."

"I've told you I don't care."

She explained. "There's a woman in Koloa—down near Poipu Beach—"

"I know where Koloa is, Glory."

It took a lot to shake Glory, but she could feel a faint blush stealing up her neck. "I'm sorry. Of course you do."

He sighed, knowing just why he had sounded so irritable. She had disturbed him for weeks, and he'd hardly seen her. Now, here, within touching distance, she was disturbing him a hundred times more. "Go on."

She nodded. "Lucy cooks in a Poipu Beach restaurant. I suggested she come here for a trial meal or two, but she says she'd rather we came there, where she's familiar with the kitchen. She thought that would be a fairer test of her skills. I'm inclined to think she's right."

"We?"

She looked up, and he saw she was frowning. "I can do it by myself, of course, if you prefer. I can't help but think that you should make this decision, though. If I hire Lucy and you don't like her cooking, we'd have to let her go. She might have trouble finding another job."

He had been about to refuse, but the truth of what she was saying stopped him. It was unlikely that he wouldn't like the woman's cooking, but the unlikely sometimes happened. "When am I supposed to perform this taste test?"

"She cooks every night from Tuesday through Saturday. She suggested we come unannounced." Glory paused. "I don't have to go. You could go alone, or with someone else. Then you could let me know what you think."

Jared leaned back, cradling the back of his head in his hands. "Do you want to go?"

She did, and she knew it had little to do with choosing a cook. She liked the idea of sitting with Jared in an intimate restaurant overlooking the ocean. She suspected she liked it too well. "If you'd like another opinion," she said carefully, "I'd be glad to give mine."

"Paradox told me you were planning to take tomorrow off."

"I was, but I didn't have any special plans."

"You were going to stay on the island?"

"I thought I'd try to find a room near one of the beaches and spend a day in the sun."

His heart did a funny little flip at the idea of Glory in a bikini, the sunlight stroking her lovely skin. "I own a cottage on Poipu." He was about to offer it to her, when a different plan coalesced. "We can take the chopper down in the morning if you'd like and spend the day there. Then we can go out to dinner in the evening."

She nodded. "And fly back tomorrow night?"

"I don't like to fly at night unless I have to. I don't worry about Dave, but there are too many barely proficient pilots on Kauai to suit me."

She realized what he was saying. "Then we'd stay until Sunday?"

Jared might have had reluctant fantasies about Glory in his arms, but he hurried to reassure her that he had no plans to turn them into reality. "It's a large cottage, with three bedrooms. There's complete privacy for both of us. You can come and go as you like." He hesitated. "If you have friends on Kauai you'd like to see, you could bring them there."

She sensed a question. "I wasn't planning to see anyone."

"If you're worried about—"

She cut him off before he could voice her concerns. "You've given me no reason to worry about anything." And he hadn't. Jared Farrell was a man who could have any woman he chose. Glory knew her own attractions, but she also knew their limitations. Jared was wealthy and powerful in his own right; he was also the scion of one of the most prominent families in the islands. She was neither wealthy nor powerful. Her family background was a proud tribute to every immigrant group who had settled Hawaii, but her forebears had been farmers and laborers. The fundamental differences between herself and Jared would keep her as safe in the Poipu Beach cottage as the presence of the rest of the staff did here at Wehilani.

Jared was already making plans. "Then I'll let Dave know when to pick us up. Is nine all right?"

"Fine." Glory stood. "I'll let you get to work."

He watched the way her very proper dress billowed around her knees as she walked away. She was the bird of paradise in a sparrow's feathers again, just as she'd been every day since they'd ridden together. He wished he could call her back and demand she wear the island styles he was sure she was most comfortable in, but he didn't. The demand would be too intimate, and in the three weeks she had been on the estate, he had resolved to avoid intimacy with her at all costs.

Which was exactly why he had just invited her to spend the night alone with him, in his moonlit, ocean-scented cottage on one of the world's most romantic beaches.

Jared ran his hand through his still-damp hair and cursed himself for a fool.

Glory had been to Poipu Beach before. Years ago her oldest brother had danced in a hula troupe that performed at the weekly luaus of several Kauai hotels. Glory had visited him and fallen in love with the island then. Poipu was only one of Kauai's marvelous beaches, and now she looked forward to having a whole day there.

She'd been looking forward to spending the day with Jared, too, until she'd realized—after an hour of trying to decide what to pack—that she was asking for trouble. Jared kindled something special in her, and it was a flame that had to be extinguished immediately unless she wanted to risk a disaster.

Once she had been honest with herself she had considered pleading a headache the next morning, or just simply telling him that she had changed her mind. He was too astute, though, to believe either story without asking incisive questions. She had committed herself to the trip, and she would go. But in the future she would be more careful. The job at Wehilani meant too much to jeopardize it by letting feelings develop for the man who would never be more than her employer.

When the next morning arrived, Glory was ready to go. She brought one small suitcase to the east wing lanai and watched Jared's helicopter materialize out of the clouds shrouding the sun. She felt, rather than heard, Jared join her. Turning to greet him, she saw that he was staring at her in the same way a man in the desert stares at an oasis.

In the brief moment before his gaze grew shuttered, she knew she wasn't alone in what she felt. Jared was drawn to her, too, and he was fighting it.

"You look ready for a day in the sun," was all he said.

She looked down at the clothing that had never seemed provocative before: the strapless lilac tube top that suddenly seemed to enhance her high breasts, the lilac-and-black sarong skirt that showed a glimpse of thigh when she moved, the black sandals that exposed every turn of her ankles and feet. Island woman all over Hawaii dressed much the same way. It was a casual, comfortable way to greet the day. Paradise was no place for plain or restrictive clothing. Even the missionaries' voluminous muumuus had been turned into colorful statements about island life.

Glory wished she was wearing one of those voluminous statements right now.

The roar of the helicopter drowned any further attempts at conversation. Jared stepped down from the lanai and motioned Glory to follow him. She bent forward and ducked her head, as he did, when she neared the helicopter's blades. Once there she let Jared help her into the seat behind Dave, the pilot, who was a soft-spoken man with a gentle smile. Jared took the seat beside him. Then, with no more motion than a bird lifting its wings to sail on the wind, they lifted off and started toward a heliport just a mile from Jared's cottage.

Glory gazed below her, savoring the sight of the island's mountain ranges, which quickly melted into square patches of taro and sugar cane. The ocean was shades of blue from turquoise to sapphire, and black lava reefs shone like polished ebony against white and golden sands.

She was sorry when the helicopter began to sink toward the ground just below them. They landed in a small, meticulously leveled field behind Dave's comfortable frame house inland from the beach. There was a small barn and a circular corral where Jared kept horses for guests who didn't want to risk the chopper or preferred to ride to Wehilani. Dave offered chopper rides to tourists when he wasn't flying for Jared, and there was a young family waiting for their turn when Jared and Glory got out. Jared took both his and

Glory's suitcases and started across the field toward a tiny parking lot surrounded by sugar cane.

Glory felt only a twinge of surprise when Jared opened the trunk of an understated black BMW convertible sitting next to the small Ford she had used when she had come to Lihue to interview potential staff. Jared dropped the suitcases inside. She let him help her into the car, leaning back against the leather cushions as she waited for him to get in.

"Slightly more comfortable than Ghost," she pronounced when they had ridden in silence for several minutes.

Jared felt tension draining from him. He had been rigid with it since he had seen her standing on the lanai, an island vision. She only needed a flower wreath on her hair and a flower lei to adorn her perfect slender shoulders.

And all he needed was a swift return of his good sense.

"What are your plans for the morning?" he asked.

"The beach, I think. I've missed it. I love the mountains, but I need to feel the ocean."

"I miss it, too. That's why I kept the cottage."

"Kept it?"

"A hotel wanted it, and all the land surrounding it. My neighbors all wanted to sell. I refused."

"Are your neighbors speaking to you?"

He laughed sardonically. "I have no neighbors. When they couldn't sell to the hotel, they sold to me, and I tore their cottages down. I own the whole point where my house sits."

She knew what beachfront property cost, but she supposed the millions Jared must have spent were inconsequential to him. It suddenly occurred to her just how alone they would be tonight.

As if to emphasize that point, Jared turned onto a narrow red clay road running off the main highway. He stopped at an iron gate blocking the road and got out of the car to unlock it. Back inside, he pulled beyond it, then got out to lock it once more. Glory waited, looking out over the sweep of land that led to the waves pounding sand the color of cream sherry. Just beyond the shore was a house, aged silver wood and sparkling glass, and surrounding the house were some of the most beautiful gardens she had ever seen.

"It's magnificent," she said, more to herself than to Jared, who was beside her once more.

"Yes, it is." He pulled into a parking space beside the house, driving slowly so that Glory could take in the view. The point was deserted except for Jared's house. There were no signs that any other buildings had existed. Palm trees swayed in the ocean breeze along the drive, and blooming poinciana, hibiscus and plumeria covered the land back up to the road as if they had grown wild there. In between, like small jewels in a lush green lawn, were gardens of other tropical flowers: anthurium, orchids, bird of paradise, set with gracefully drooping ferns. One garden was varying species of cacti, another was bromeliads, their exotic, otherworldly foliage a contrast for riotously colored spikes of blooms.

"I didn't want a hotel here," Jared said as Glory took in the lush tropical landscape. "I don't know if that was selfish or farsighted. It's a question I ask myself every day." He seemed to pull himself back from somewhere far away. "My caretaker lives up the road. Everything should be ready for us. If you find anything that seems to have been overlooked, let me know."

Fleetingly she wondered how many times the caretaker had been called on to get the beach estate—she could no longer think of it as a cottage—ready for Jared and a woman guest. She reminded herself that she was not a guest; she was Jared's employee and nothing more. He had generously volunteered to give her a memorable day off. That was all.

"Is there anything else I can do while I'm here?" she asked.

Jared was getting out of the car, but he turned at her words and frowned. "Yes, you can relax and have fun. You're here as my guest, not my estate manager."

She realized she would have felt more comfortable as manager. She smiled anyway. He was unexpectedly generous. "Thank you."

Jared wondered if she knew what her smiles did to a man. Most women seemed to learn about smiles at their mothers' knee. Patsy, he suspected, had figured it out in the womb. But Glory's smiles were different somehow. They came from deep inside her, with no calculation. It was like a light, an inner light, being turned on, and even when she wasn't smiling, the light still glowed warmly in her eyes.

He realized the danger of the path his thoughts were taking, and he covered up his irritation with gruffness. "I'll show you where you'll be staying."

Outside the car, the air was fragrant with the smells that meant home to Glory. She drew in a deep breath and let the salty tang of the ocean and the sweet scent of plumeria fill her lungs; then she followed Jared, who was taking their suitcases inside.

"Can I swim here?" she asked.

"I'll show you the best place, and if you like snorkeling, there's a reef just down from the house that's excellent."

"I'd like that."

The interior of the house was as lovely and unpretentious as its exterior. It had been designed for comfort and to provide views of the incomparable landscape. Here there were no fussy antiques, no priceless works of art. Much of the furniture was rattan, with tropical print upholstery, and windows provided the major adornments on the light wood walls.

Jared led Glory to a bedroom and bath at the end of the hallway. "I think you'll be comfortable here," he said, setting her suitcase inside.

The room was spacious and airy, with white wicker furniture and fresh flower arrangements that complemented the soft lavender-and-turquoise print of the bedspread and chair cushions. Best of all there was a glass door leading to a private lanai overlooking the ocean.

Glory's eyes sparkled when she turned to Jared. "I'll be more than comfortable. I feel like a princess."

Jared had convinced himself that he would leave her here after pointing out the reef and the swimming beach from her lanai. Now he found that he couldn't. She was radiant with enthusiasm, and her radiance was magnetic. He was drawn to her, and he had no desire to leave. He realized that he wanted to see the beauty of the beach through her eyes. He wanted to watch her excitement.

He wanted to watch *her*.

"I'm glad you like it." Jared was uncomfortably aware of how close they were standing. He wanted to reach out and finger a long lock of hair that had escaped from the thick mass piled on her head. Better yet, he wanted to pull the pins and watch it all tumble down her back. He reined in his imagination before it could progress to the next logical step. "Are you planning to go down to the beach after you change?"

"I thought I would." Glory realized she had stopped breathing. Jared was so close that she could have leaned forward and fallen into his arms.

"I'll come, too, and show you where the reef is."

"Good." Glory watched Jared's eyes darken from brown to stormy black. Was the lack of air making her light-headed, or was it something even more elemental, something that was affecting him, too?

Jared forced himself to move away. "Get ready," he said over his shoulder. "I'll meet you outside."

"Fine." The word was almost too soft to hear.

There was nothing subtle about Glory's body. In a bikini it was every man's dream and every puritan's nightmare. Jared had known to expect the firm, high breasts, the impossibly narrow waist, the flaring hips and long shapely legs. He had known, too, that like any island woman with the right figure, she would wear a bikini. What he hadn't known was how it would affect him.

She was exquisite, and he was a man. It was that simple, and that complicated. He was only glad that he had immersed himself in the water while she unwrapped the pareu that had covered her suit. Now he swam into the waves and let the cool water and salt spray calm his reaction.

Glory refused snorkeling equipment, swimming out to the reef without it to watch the fish without benefit of a mask. Jared went with her to savor the rainbow colors: the yellow and black butterfish; the iridescent turquoise parrot fish; the royal blue of the Achilles Tang. There were others, too, polka-dotted, striped and colored in hues too brilliant to have names. Jared watched the fish, but more often he watched Glory, her hair streaming behind her in a floating dark cloud, her body cutting through the water with the grace of a dolphin.

Glory was acutely aware of Jared, too. She had grown up with brothers and cousins who more often than not wore ragged cutoff jeans and nothing more. Seeing Jared in black knit swim trunks was very different. She was used to men with solid, muscular physiques, but she wasn't used to Jared's long, perfect limbs, the breadth of his shoulders, the narrow width of his hips.

Growing up, she had thought she would never want a man enough to give up the hard-won opportunity for privacy. She had seen friends marry before they were twenty to bear children and begin a life much like that of their parents, and she hadn't understood why. Now she was beginning to understand, although she understood something else: her friends had been smarter than she'd thought. They had chosen men they had everything in common with. They had not chosen men like Jared Farrell.

Through their long, tiring swim, she and Jared never touched, as if he were as afraid as she to risk contact. When they finally emerged from the water they lay side by side on a wide beach blanket, still not touching, to let the sun dry them.

Later, her blue-and-red pareu covering the lush curves of her body, Glory wandered through the gardens, picking flowers to tuck into her hair. Jared had gone inside to change, and she was alone. The sun had disappeared behind clouds, and she could see silver sheets of rain on the horizon.

She wanted to watch the storm come in. The wind was already torturing the poinciana trees, scattering their vermillion blossoms across the sand and over the whitecapped surf. Glory sat on a stone bench, hidden by the chest-high border of a hedge and watched the storm move closer.

The surf was being whipped back from the sand as if it had struck an invisible barrier, when she heard Jared calling her name.

"I'm over here," she called, standing to show him.

Jared strode across the lawn. "I was starting to get worried. This should blow over in a little while, but we've been known to get winds high enough to knock over trees on this point. We get the worst buffeting from every direction here."

"I'll go inside in a minute," she promised. "It's just so lovely. The rain's almost here."

Reluctantly he sat beside her. He wanted to be sure she went inside if the wind grew dangerous. She was only inches away, and she was gazing at her hands. As he watched, she twisted two tiny blossoms, intermingling them, then wrenching them apart in a poignant pas de deux.

"What are you doing?" He reached down and lightly grasped her hands. He lifted the flowers to see them more clearly. Each white blossom seemed to be only half-formed. They were tiny, the size of violets, and delicately fringed along the edge. "I've never seen these before," he said as Glory put them in his hand.

"You've seen them, but you've never noticed them." She turned and reached into the shrub beside her. She removed two flowers, identical to the ones she had given him. "See?" She held them out to him. "This is naupaka. It's common enough, but most of the time we just notice the shrub, not the bloom."

"What were you doing with them?"

She smiled, but there was something wistful about the look she gave him. "Don't you know the legend?"

"Apparently not. I didn't even know the flower."

Glory held one flower in each hand. "Once there was an island girl from a poor family. She was beautiful, and men fell in love with her the first time they saw her. A mountain king came down to the beaches where the girl lived, and he fell in love with her, too. With purest devotion the girl gave her heart to the king, but because he was royalty and she a commoner, they could never be together. The king went back to his mountain, and the girl stayed in the village below. She waits for him, still. The naupaka tells the story."

Glory brought the blossoms together until they were almost touching. "Each blossom is only half-developed, just as the king and his true love are only half-alive because they can't be together. Only when they are united will the naupaka grow into one perfect flower." She brought the flowers together and linked them. They appeared to be one.

The first raindrops fell before Jared could respond. Glory stood, dropping the tiny blossoms at her feet. "I don't mind getting wet, but I'll make you wet, too, unless we go inside."

Jared rose, but as Glory turned toward the house, he rested a hand on her shoulder. "Perhaps the king wasn't worth the young woman's love. If he had been, he would have claimed her despite their differences."

"Some things are impossible, I think. Sometimes love is impossible."

"Not impossible, inadvisable."

She smiled sadly. "It's a shame you weren't there to tell that to the young woman and the king. I can still feel their suffering. Can't you?"

She was gone, running through the rain up to the house, before he could respond. He unclasped his hand and saw the two blossoms that she had given him. They lay crushed on his palm, separated, like the beautiful girl and the king. He closed his hand once more, and when he opened it, the two flowers clung to each other as raindrops splashed against his skin. One flower. United.

Jared was thoroughly soaked before he realized that he was still standing in the rain, staring at the naupaka. He flipped his hand over and watched the flowers, still united, drift to the ground. Then he turned and ran up the path to the house.

Chapter Five

Glory examined herself in the wall mirror against the closet door. She had brought only one dress with her, a strapless white sundress that fit tightly at the bodice and then flared, princess style, to just below her knees. The simplicity of the design complemented her figure, and the stark white enhanced the creamy tint of her skin. She had the vague feeling, however, that she looked like a bird plucked of its plumage. She had intended to string a simple lei to add color to the dress, but the rain had come before she could choose the flowers. Although the storm had been short, the wind had scattered many blossoms, and the rain had bruised and soaked what had been left. She contented herself with a short strand of delicate ivory-tinted shells and left her hair down for contrast.

Jared was waiting for her in the living room, looking out over the ocean at the sun that was just beginning to set around the edge of the point. He turned when she entered, and his gaze traveled over her. "You look lovely."

She smiled. "Thank you. I've never seen you in an aloha shirt before." She admired the tropical print with its black background and many-hued flowers. "Very nice."

"Aren't we pretending to be tourists tonight?"

"To fool Lucy? She'll be in the kitchen, anyway. She won't know who's out front."

"She's sure to have her spies. I think we'd better play the game." He turned and lifted a long white box off a table by the window. "This is for you. A disguise."

Glory moved closer and accepted the box. She lifted the top and examined the contents. When she raised her eyes to his, they were glowing. "It's beautiful, Jared. This is a real work of art." She set the box on the table and lifted out a lei that featured a variety of flowers in hues of red, white and pink woven together with delicate fronds of lace fern. The sweet fragrance of gardenia and ginger wafted through the air.

"My caretaker's wife made it. She's won a number of blue ribbons on lei day."

"I can understand why." Glory saw that Jared was frowning as if he didn't know what had come over him. Behind the frown she saw something that looked very much like self-doubt. "Thank you," she said, stepping closer to him. She held out the lei. "Will you put it on for me?"

Jared knew the custom. He had given Glory the lei, but the ritual wouldn't be complete until he slipped it over her head. He was curiously reluctant to perform the simple act. The lines in their relationship were already blurred. He wondered if they would even exist after he set the lei on her shoulders and lifted her black waterfall of hair over it.

He took the lei anyway. His palms grazed her cheeks as he lowered it over her head. Then he filled his hands with the silken bounty of her hair and pulled it from beneath the lei until it was free. He released it and watched it flow down her back.

The time had come to step back, to smile and say they should go. But Jared couldn't. His arms still encircled her, and his fingers lingered in her hair. Finally he let his hands glide down the length of it until they were resting lightly on each side of the flowers adorning her shoulders. She was gazing up at him, no smile on her lovely features. She seemed to be waiting, too, and he knew that for once her serenity had vanished.

His fingers tightened on her shoulders, and he leaned forward to brush a kiss across her forehead. Her skin was warm and smooth. He wanted to linger there, to taste her again, to feel her arms slide around his waist to hold him. He wanted . . .

He stepped back. "Aloha." His hands fell to his sides.

"Aloha," she said huskily.

He didn't move away. The fragrance of the lei drifted in the air between them. Something else moved between them, too. *I don't want this,* he seemed to say, although no words were spoken.

I didn't want this, either, she silently agreed. *But there's no changing what's happening, is there?*

Jared wasn't sure how long they stood that way. Time seemed to have little meaning until the soft chiming of the mantel clock forced him back to reality. He stiffened, fully aware for the first time of just how vulnerable he had let himself become. "We'd better go."

Glory heard the edge to his voice, and she knew what had put it there. She smiled sadly. "Yes, we'd better. Our reservations will be gone if we don't hurry."

The restaurant where Lucy Ho cooked was a small battered board building that stood beside the road winding along the Poipu coast. The building was unpretentious, but one look at the assorted clientele satisfied Glory that the food would be excellent. Apparently the Beach Hut had yet to be discovered by tourists, but Kauai's year-round residents had given it their stamp of approval. The guests so obviously enjoying their food were locals, calling back and forth across the room to each other and bouncing children on their knees.

Glory examined Jared from the corner of her eye to see how he was taking the casual chatter. She had expected something a little more formal. Jared, she imagined, had expected something on a par with some of the island's best restaurants. To her surprise he was peering down at the floor, a grin contorting the usually serious lines of his face.

At his feet, a tiny toddler girl, all shining black hair and ruffled diapers, was untying his shoes. A harried waitress stalked by, shaking her head as she saw Jared's predicament. She yelled something in Chinese, and one of the customers looked up, aghast. In a moment the young mother had recaptured her child and rattled off an apology in beautifully accented English.

The harried waitress appeared moments later and led them to a table facing the ocean—or, rather, facing the highway that edged along the beach. They stared out the dust-streaked window whose major view was the cars cruising the highway, and then turned their chairs the required distance to block it out.

"I'll bet the food's good," Glory said, hoping her prediction was correct.

Jared knew she was embarrassed. Before he'd even thought about what he was doing, he'd covered her folded hands with one of his. "If it's as enjoyable as the atmosphere, this will be a perfect evening."

She smiled gratefully. "I suppose if Lucy were cooking at the Westin or the Waiohai, she wouldn't want to change jobs, would she?"

Jared lifted his hand and reached for his water glass. "Why *does* she want to change?" He inclined his head toward the other patrons. "She's obviously got an appreciative audience here."

"She wants to cook for smaller numbers. She says she likes to experiment, and she doesn't get the opportunity because she's too busy. If you want my opinion, I think she's just tired of the rat race."

"Any family?"

"Not to speak of. A daughter who lives on the mainland, and a sister who lives on Maui. Lucy seems to be ready for a little peace and quiet. She'll keep her house here for her days off."

Jared nodded. "Sounds good."

"I hope so."

Jared sat back, his eyes never leaving Glory's face. The waitress arrived, and after asking for her opinion, they ordered a variety of dishes to sample. Jared waited until she had gone before he spoke.

"You know, you don't have to work so hard to convince me you can do your job."

Glory knew he had picked up her insecurities. She tried to cover them. "Don't I? Aren't you the man who was going to fire me just because I turned out to be a young woman?"

He ignored the challenge. "I'm still surprised you want the job. You could make the same salary working for one of the big hotels, and you'd have the chance for a social life, too."

"But I don't want a social life." The words were out before she realized she was going to have to explain them. She wasn't ready to share her dream with Jared. The only people who knew about her book were her family, who loved her, and Toby and Cole, who also loved her. She wasn't ready to give anyone more objective the chance to take her stories and drawings and criticize them. The book was her heart and soul, and she knew that if it was dismissed as worthless, she might never recover.

"Have you been hurt?" Jared asked. His mouth drew into a grim line at the thought. For all her serenity, Glory seemed to have an innocence that could make her a target for a man who was only looking for a beautiful woman to pass the time with.

"I'm tough," she teased. "Unbelievably tough. Men run when they see me coming. No one can get close enough to hurt me. They're too scared."

He laughed derisively. "As tough as one of those flowers you're wearing?"

She looked down at her lei. "Any one of these flowers had to survive incredible odds to end up here. They're tough, all right."

"And have you survived incredible odds?"

"In a way, I suppose." She didn't want to bore Jared with family stories, but he seemed interested. She compromised and told him a little. "My father died when I was ten. There were a lot of children to support and not much money to do it with. My mother's a strong woman. She did what she could, but she couldn't do it alone. We all pitched in. I've worked every kind of job you can imagine, from dancing in a hula troupe to selling sandwiches at a Bonsai Pipeline lunch wagon when the surf was up. Sometimes I did both and cleaned hotel rooms, too. If that's surviving, then I'm all for it, because I learned something that most girls don't. I don't need anyone to take care of me. I can take care of myself."

Jared wondered how much of what she said was true. He had no reason to doubt her story, but he'd had no reason to doubt Patsy, either, or the other women who had traveled through his life. "So you're not looking for a man? And Wehilani doesn't seem too quiet for you?"

She imagined the truth would be impossible for him to understand, but she tried anyway. "Quiet is something I've dreamed about most of my life. You'll never know what it means to me."

His response was interrupted by the arrival of their waitress with the appetizers they had ordered. By the time she left, Glory was ready to change the subject.

"I'd love to know the history of Wehilani." She reached for a marinated mushroom. "Sally's told me a little, but she tends to embellish."

"She serves up the story with considerable drama," he agreed. "But there's nothing wonderful about it. My forefathers thought they'd like to own an island or two. They bought every bit of Kauai they could afford, which was a tremendous amount considering the pennies they were willing to pay for it. Then they proceeded to cheat their way to owning more."

Glory was surprised he was so frank—and so cynical. "That was a long time ago. They weren't the only ones who exploited the Hawaiian people."

"Not the only ones, certainly, but by the time they were done, they'd done their fair share. They didn't own Kauai, but they owned enough to pretend they did. I suppose all that wheeling and dealing was exhausting, so the next generation built a family retreat and called it Wehilani. To their credit, Wehilani wasn't really land anyone else was anxious to own. The Hawaiian people had vacated their villages in the mountains and valleys long before the Farrells decided to buy an island. Life was easier close to the ocean."

"And so your family built the house and cleared the grounds?"

"My great-great-grandfather was responsible for that. He lived at Wehilani for a year, then decided it was too isolated. No one else has ever lived there year-round. It was a seldom used hideaway until I bought it from the family corporation."

"You must have had some good memories of time spent there to want to own it."

Jared reached for a thin strip of tuna that had been marinated with the mushrooms. "There were no good memories."

Glory knew better than to pry. Jared's expression made that quite clear. "And still you bought it," she said, leaving room for him to say more if he chose.

"I bought it to keep it safe," he said. "The family was going to divide it. They were already negotiating with the state to build a highway. There were plans for condominiums and hotels. Wehilani would have become an exclusive resort."

It was the second time that day that he'd talked about stopping development on land he owned. And she had seen his reaction to the minor threat the backpackers had represented. Glory couldn't decide whether he was a conservationist or just one of a breed of people willing to spend millions to keep the world's beauty for their own private pleasure. There was no polite way to ask.

"Are there good memories now?" she asked instead. "Do you like living there, Jared?"

"It suits me. I've come to terms with the ghosts."

She didn't know what to say to that. They finished the rest of the appetizers in silence.

The main course was succulent local fish, mahi mahi for Glory and ono for Jared, accompanied by a medley of crisp steamed vegetables covered in a delicate sweet-and-sour sauce. Dessert was lilikoi chiffon pie, a passion-fruit-flavored pastry that was so light it almost floated off their forks.

"Well?" Glory asked as she watched Jared savor his last bite.

"If you think she'll fit in with the rest of the staff, hire her."

"Good." Glory pulled a pad out of her handbag and wrote a note, slipping it into an envelope that already had Lucy's name on it. When the waitress appeared to present the bill to Jared, Glory handed the envelope to her and asked that it be delivered to Lucy.

Outside, the sky was a brilliant canopy of stars. A hotel nearby was having a luau for their guests, and the soothing sound of slack key guitars and love ballads filled the air. Glory swayed to the music, not even aware that she did. She hummed the melody as she gazed up at the sky.

Jared listened with more interest. His knowledge of the Hawaiian language was minimal. Now he wished he knew more. Glory had a faraway gleam in her eyes, and her body moving to the music was grace itself. When the song had finished he spoke.

"What was the song about?"

For a moment Glory had almost forgotten where she was. She had been transported to another time when life was simpler and the love of a man and woman was expressed in song without benefit of screaming vocalists and profane lyrics.

She smiled enigmatically. "It's very simple, really. A man tells a woman she is like the moon rising, like the sound of a seabird in a lonely night, like the perfect blossoms that carpet the path to her hut. He asks her if he may lie with her, and she answers that he is like the sun rising in a morning sky, the triumphant call of the albatross as it conquers the ocean's breadth, the rare tree that thrives on the side of the steepest mountain."

"I gather that means yes?"

She laughed. "Ah, now *that* I won't tell you."

"Then you speak Hawaiian?"

"I know our songs and chants, and the commoner words and phrases. My mother tried to teach us what she knew, and we dot our English with Hawaiian at home to keep in practice, but each generation loses a little. I wanted to go to the university to study. . . ." She paused, then shook her head again. "But it just wasn't possible."

"You're not too old."

"But I am too employed," she said with another laugh. "I study on my own, and that suits me right now."

Jared touched her arm lightly to guide her to the car. He thought of all the women he had known who had been given everything and had done nothing except demand more. If what Glory said was true, she was their mirror image, a young woman who had been given little and done everything she could with it.

If what she said was true.

Jared dropped his hand to his side. Distrust was too ingrained in him to abandon. On the surface Glory was everything fine and good. But Patsy had appeared much the same way at first, and so had the other women he'd known. He was more than careful now; he was suspicious. He was not a man searching for love, or even for a lover. He was a man who had made his peace with loneliness.

But if that was true, why did he want to take Glory Kalia in his arms and make her both his lover and his true love? She was beautiful, but she had no monopoly on beauty. She was intelligent, but she had no monopoly there, either. He wondered if the Hawaiian moon was destroying his sharply honed survival instincts.

"It's such a beautiful night." Glory stopped at the car door and gazed up at the sky again. "It rains more here than it does at home. A clear night like this is a pleasure."

"Would you like to drive along the coast for a while? If we go far enough to the west we might see Niihau."

"The Forbidden Island." From the helicopter, Glory had seen the small island off Kauai's coast, owned by the descendants of a woman who, like Jared's ancestors, had wanted to own an island. Unlike the Farrells, Elizabeth Sinclair had succeeded. For the grand sum of $10,000 she had purchased the entire island from King Kamehameha V in 1864. Today Niihau was forbidden to anyone other than family members and the people of pure Hawaiian descent who lived and worked there, much as they had a century before. "I'd like to see it at night," she answered. "It's the island of mystery." She gave in to impulse. "And could we put the top down?"

Jared opened her door. "Why not?"

Once they were out of the Poipu area, the road became less crowded. With the convertible's top down, the stars seemed to be only an arm's length away. They passed beachside estates and more modest homes inland, all with blooming gardens that sent their sweet fragrances to perfume the warm tropical night.

Glory and Jared drove most of the way in silence. Wehilani and the exclusive areas of Poipu beach were only a small part of the real Kauai. Here, farther from the tourist throngs, was the Kauai where people worked and wept, played and worshiped their God. Here were towns with PTA meetings and Red Cross classes, farmers' markets and Saturday night dances.

"This feels like home." Glory pointed at a small white board church with a spire pointing the way to heaven. "Our church looks a lot like that one. On Wednesday nights they'll have a quilting party, and on alternate Fridays they'll have a covered-dish supper. The quilt they're working on will have Hawaiian motifs, and someone's bound to bring octopus and poi to the supper, but other than that, if you attend, you'll think you're in Kansas."

"Never." Jared negotiated a sharp curve as he spoke. "And may it never be so."

"You don't like Kansas?" she teased.

"Kansas should be Kansas. Hawaii should be Hawaii."

They slipped back into silence until he slowed to a stop in a sandy plot of ground beside a pasture. She was surprised when he got out and came around to open her door.

"Infinity." He opened the door and held it for her.

She got out, waiting for him to explain. Jared turned and began to walk along the side of the road, leading her to a path that hadn't been visible from the car. They walked side by side through the pasture, not progressing very far before Glory could hear the crashing of waves. They passed through a small grove of trees where broken limbs had been captured by vines and grasses to make otherworldly sculptures, then onto a beach of golden sand.

"Infinity Beach." Jared gestured toward the stretch of sand and water whose waves broke and receded in a passionate ballet, sending glistening wreaths of spray to meet the evening air.

"Lovely. Perfect." Glory kicked off her sandals to feel the cool sand between her toes. She dragged her feet as if she were skating as she made her way to the water's edge. "Look at the waves, Jared. They're dancing!"

He hadn't expected such uninhibited joy. The spot had always been a favorite of his. He had been brought here often by the one person in his childhood who had loved him without reserve or qualification. Then, when he'd thought he was falling in love with Patsy, he had brought her here to share it with her. She had given lip service to its beauty, but she hadn't wanted to linger. Sand and sea spray couldn't compete with the island's more civilized attractions.

"*You're* dancing," Jared said, coming up behind Glory, who was swaying to the rhythm of the ocean. "You look like you're going to throw yourself into the waves."

"I wish I could, but it's a little cold for that."

The sky was bright enough that Jared could see goose bumps on Glory's bare arms. "You should have told me you were cold. We can go. I'll put the top up on the car."

She whirled around. "Oh, I don't want to go, not yet. I'll be fine. Could we walk a little ways?"

He was doubtful, but he couldn't refuse. He inclined his head to the right. "That way's the best. The waves bring thousands of shells up to the shore."

She started along beside him. "Are you a beachcomber, then?"

"As a child I was."

She repressed a shiver and made a silent vow to bring a sweater the next time she went walking along a Kauai beach.

Jared glanced at her and caught just the faintest tremor. Without weighing the pros and cons, he pulled her close, tucking her under the shelter of his arm. "Better?"

Better for what? Better for whom? "Mmm... yes," she murmured noncommittally.

He knew just what the "mmm..." meant. They were alone on the beach. The islanders came here to swim and fish for pompano, to collect shells and watch the waves, but, as if they had made a secret pact to give the beach to Glory and Jared, they were all absent tonight.

Glory fit perfectly against him, her body curving provocatively against his. He could smell the ginger and gardenia sweetness of the lei and the fresh, clean scent of her hair. He had made silent vows not to touch her; he had reminded himself of past hurts and broken promises. And still, as if the past had never existed and vows had never been said, he held her to his side as if they were lovers.

They didn't speak again until they were almost at the bend where the beach ended. Each moment of holding her close had sensitized Jared to the feel of her skin, the lush warmth of her body, the smell of gardenias and ginger. He was glad the torturous walk was half-finished.

Glory was glad, too. She had walked on moonlit beaches with men before, but she had never been affected this way. Jared's arm around her seemed the most profound of intimacies. It was too much and much too little. She was confused, and she was frightened of both the feelings he generated and the response she might give.

"Can you see Niihau?" Jared raised the arm that wasn't around her shoulders and pointed. "There, in the distance."

Glory couldn't see the island; the night, even brightly lit by stars, was too dark for that. But she could see a shadow on the horizon. As she stared, the shadow seemed to grow darker, thicker. "I think I see it," she said. "But maybe I just want to."

"I've been there."

Glory was surprised. She had never met anyone who had been allowed on the Forbidden Island. "What's it like?"

"Very different from here. Flatter, hotter. The whole island's a sheep and cattle ranch. The workers live in wooden houses without electricity or any of what we call modern conveniences. Then, every October, everyone stops work to comb the beaches for shells to make leis to sell here and on the other islands."

Glory had seen the leis, which were so intricate and delicate that they could sell for well over a thousand dollars. She knew the people who made them discarded most of the tiny shells they found, choosing only the most perfect, which they pierced with the sharpened spokes of a bicycle wheel before they strung them. The leis were looked on with awe, and the people of Niihau who had made them seemed to have a mysterious aura, a people out of time.

"Why were you there?" she asked.

"I know some members of the family. We have a continuing dialogue about past and present, rights and responsibilities."

She waited, but he said no more. He just turned her so that he could see her face. They were standing so close that she could read the mixture of wariness and longing in his eyes.

She knew he wouldn't speak of what he was feeling. She couldn't admit her own feelings, either. The flickering flame of their attraction needed only a word to set it raging out of control. Glory knew there would be nothing left to salvage when the flame died out. They were wrong for each other, as mismatched as the island girl and her mountain king.

She couldn't speak, but she realized she wanted very much to let him know she understood his confusion and felt it, too. She lifted her hand and touched his cheek. He shut his eyes as she drew her fingertips slowly to his jaw. Her hand trembled as she savored the warmth of his smoothly shaven cheek.

She dropped her hand and moved away until they stood side by side once more. "Thank you for a beautiful day," she said, no longer able to look at him.

"You're welcome."

"When I'm back at Wehilani, I'll think of this place."

Jared wanted to pull Glory back into his arms and to shove her away. She had gotten too close, yet she seemed too distant. Again, he cursed himself for a fool. He cursed the night ahead when they would lie quietly, rooms apart, and wish they were in each other's arms.

"I think we'd better get back," he said, betraying none of his feelings. "I told Dave we'd be flying home early tomorrow."

With his arm just grazing her shoulders now, they started toward the car. Glory thought about the room Jared had chosen for her. It suddenly seemed too large and too empty. Solitude, the thing she had wished for most in her life, now seemed curiously undesirable.

They were almost to the rocky point that divided the beach when Glory felt a sharp pain in the sole of her foot. She gave a soft cry and stopped, lifting her foot to peer down at a small gash that turned red in the moonlight as she watched.

"You've cut it," Jared said, crouching to examine her foot. He felt along the sand until he'd found what he was looking for. He held up part of a broken bottle for her to see.

"I knew it wasn't anything nature made. I'm used to shells," she said, holding on to Jared's shoulder and leaning down to brush the sand from her foot. "It's just a small cut. My sandals are right over there. Would you get them for me?"

Jared stood, giving her time to catch her balance before he destroyed it completely. He swept her into his arms and started toward the car.

"Jared, I can—"

"Shh . . ." he commanded.

"It's just a tiny—"

"I said shh. . . ."

"I can walk."

He stopped and looked down at her. Her hair trailed almost to the sand, and her lei lay crushed between them, perfuming the air. She was frowning, but whether it was from pain or humiliation, he didn't know. He smiled grimly. "Do you think this has anything to do with whether you can walk or not?"

She stopped frowning, stopped protesting. She slid her arms around his neck and lay quietly against his chest until they reached the car, where Jared lifted her over the door and set her gently inside. He let go of her by reluctant degrees, then straightened and went back to the beach to retrieve her sandals.

He said nothing when he returned; he just started the car and headed toward Poipu Beach. Glory sat beside him and wished that the few moments in his arms could have lasted all night.

Chapter Six

After their return to Wehilani, Jared stayed only long enough to finish some paperwork and have his suitcases packed for a trip to Detroit to meet with two major automakers. Then on Monday he was gone with little more than an abrupt nod to Glory, who was waiting on the lanai, and instructions on where he could be reached in an emergency.

It was almost as if the intimacy of their interlude together had never existed. As the helicopter flew out of sight, Glory told herself that Jared's departure was for the best. Now she could concentrate on her job and her book, and she could put all errant thoughts of him out of her mind. But she knew the saying Easier Said Than Done had been coined for times like this.

"Seems like these days he's gone more than he's here."

Glory hadn't heard Sally come up behind her. She turned to see the housekeeper shaking her head morosely, as if she'd just heard that a neighbor had died. "He'll be back in two weeks," Glory assured her, trying not to smile.

"I've known Jared Farrell since he was a little boy. He doesn't like the mainland. He won't be happy there."

"For two weeks?"

"He doesn't go unless he has to. Bad memories."

Glory wrestled with her conscience. She knew she had no business asking Sally about Jared's personal history, and yet she wanted to understand him. He was a mystery to her; all she really knew was that she was dangerously close to falling in love with him.

Conscience gave way to curiosity. "What kind of memories?" she asked, following Sally inside to the kitchen. Lucy was arriving at the end of the week, and Sally was determined that every square inch of the room and appliances would be scrubbed and polished before she did.

"He was raised on the mainland, in New Jersey. His parents were—" Sally abruptly cut herself off, raising her eyes to heaven as if seeking an apology for her thoughts.

"What were you going to say?" Glory prompted.

"I started working for Mr. and Mrs. Farrell when I was twenty," Sally said. She went to the sink and turned on the faucets to fill it with hot water. She searched the cabinets beneath and pulled out a strong disinfectant, which she added to the hot water. In a moment the kitchen smelled like a hospital.

Glory's eyes began to burn, but she wanted to know about Jared more than she wanted to escape.

"As I was saying, I started—"

"Working for Mr. and Mrs. Farrell when you were twenty," Glory repeated. "Go on, please, Sally."

"They were cold and mean, rich as kings but the worst kind of penny-pinchers. I wouldn't have stayed on, but right after I got there, Mrs. Farrell got pregnant with Jared. She cried and carried on like it was life-threatening or something!"

Glory wondered if Jared's mother had taught Sally her own dramatic responses. "So you stayed so she wouldn't have to hire someone new?"

"That's right. Though why I bothered trying to please a woman who couldn't be pleased is anybody's guess. Anyhow, when Jared was born, I knew right away that someone had to be there to make sure that poor child got some love. I'd started going out with Rolfe by then, and I wasn't anxious to leave him, anyway. I tried to be sure Jared was taken care of, but the Farrells didn't want me near him. They hired a snooty baby nurse who was as cold as they were. I'd hear that baby crying, and no one would pick him up. Sometimes, when no one was around, I'd sneak in his room and cuddle him. It was our secret."

Glory couldn't imagine anyone raising a child the way Sally was describing. There hadn't been extra space in her house, and there hadn't been silence, but there had always been someone to hold her when she cried.

She tried to sound objective. "That must have been hard for you."

"Hard for Jared, you mean! He was a brilliant little boy, a son anyone would be proud of, but his mother and father were never proud of him. He wasn't allowed to be a child. They weren't really religious people, you know, the kind that have God in here." She beat her chest. "But they used religion to frighten him. They used anything they could to frighten him, just so he'd behave the way they wanted. If he weren't the person he is, he'd be scared of everything now. But Jared's not scared of anything because he was too smart for them. He got away as soon as he was old enough to walk out the door."

"How did he do that?"

"He had a great-aunt who lived here on Kauai, down at the beach house where you stayed Saturday. She saw what was happening to him, and she was a good woman—really good, you know what I mean?"

For once Sally had dropped the dramatics. The story had enough power on its own. Glory nodded to encourage her and touched her own chest. "The kind of goodness that comes from in here?"

Sally smiled. "You understand. Anyway, Mr. and Mrs. Farrell went to Europe when Jared was twelve, and they sent him to stay with Mr. Farrell's aunt, Janet. Right before Jared was due to go back to New Jersey, she and him had a long talk. I guess he told her the truth about his parents, because she decided she couldn't let him go back to them. So when the Farrells returned and sent for him, Janet just said no. Then she used her ace in the hole. She told them that if they'd leave Jared with her, she'd will all her holdings on the island and all her money to Jared when she died."

"And that worked?"

"She was an old woman, and she had health problems. I guess Jared's father thought she'd croak any day, and he saw a chance to get his hands on even more money and land. So he agreed. Rolfe and I quit working for them the day we found out they'd sold their son. When Janet Farrell discovered we'd left Jared's parents, she hired us to come to Kauai to work for her."

The story stunned Glory. She couldn't even imagine parents as heartless as Sally had described. "Did Jared ever go back to live with his parents?" she asked, hoping the answer was no.

"He went back for visits, though as seldom as possible. He'd come back to the island, and he'd be real quiet for weeks, like he was working something out in his head. Then he'd brighten up, little by little. In those days the whole Farrell family got together for Thanksgiving here, at Wehilani, every year. He'd see his parents then, too, because they felt they had to come to protect their interests in the family corporation. But they never came any other time. They didn't really care if they saw their son or not!"

"They must have had some feelings for him." Glory wanted to believe they had. She couldn't fathom anyone as selfish or cruel as Sally was making Jared's parents out to be.

Sally snorted in response. "Janet died when Jared was eighteen, like she'd hung on all those years just to be sure he was safe from having to go back to New Jersey. She left Jared everything she had, and she made it impossible for his father to touch any of it. Mr. and Mrs. Farrell blamed it all on Jared. They told him he was on his own. They didn't want anything to do with him again."

Glory didn't know what to say. Her eyes stung from more than the smell of ammonia. She just shook her head. Sally must have thought that was response enough.

"Jared's father died a couple of years ago. The funny thing is that after all his penny-pinching and cheating other people, he died broke. He'd sold all his land in the islands and invested the money in a couple of schemes that went under. So now Jared supports his mother. She never calls or writes, and she never visits. Jared sends her money and calls her regularly, but he doesn't expect anything from her. He does it because she's his mother. He's a good man, loyal, even when he shouldn't be."

Glory thought of Jared's concern for Hugh and silently agreed. But he was also a moody man, and now she understood his moods a little better. He had survived the cruel treatment of his parents, but he hadn't survived unscathed. "I shouldn't have asked you all this," she admitted, "but I'm glad I know more about Jared now."

"You know, it's a funny thing." Sally had scrubbed all the countertops as she'd talked. Now she progressed to the stove. "There are some who'd say Jared Farrell is the luckiest man alive. He inherited a fortune, then made another one. Chances are he'll make a few more before he's done. He lives like a king on a mountaintop, and he owns a good chunk of the island below. But he's not a lucky man. The only person he was ever really close to died when he was just eighteen. And not one of the women who've thrown themselves at him has been good enough to tie his shoes."

Glory had the sudden image of a baby girl with ruffled diapers who had joyfully *untied* Jared's shoes. She remembered his grin, and she suddenly realized just how much love he had to give. A lifetime's worth. He would be a wonderful father and husband—for the right woman.

Sally looked up, and her eyes took on a crafty gleam. "At least he's got a staff that cares about him," she said. "We all think the world of Jared. You're new, but you like him, too, don't you, Glory?"

Glory knew a leading question when she heard one. "It's not really my place to like him or not, is it? He's my employer."

Sally didn't even pretend to be hurt. "Everyone has an opinion. Jared sure has his about you."

Glory didn't ask what it was. She knew she was going to be told anyway.

"His eyes follow you everywhere you go."

"Sally, I don't think this is—"

"He wants to think you're too good to be true. It'd be safer."

Glory felt heat rising in her cheeks. "Sally—"

"But you're not. Everyone here likes you. . . ." Sally opened the oven door and, with her head inside, began to scrub. "Especially Jared."

Glory wasn't sure if she'd heard the housekeeper's closing remark or just imagined it.

In the first week of Jared's absence Glory worked with Rolfe, supervising the restoration of the outside trim. A work crew from Lihue was flown up every day to restain and seal the beautiful wood, which had come from Wehilani's own forests. When they finished, the outbuildings—Jared's lab, the gazebo, the stables and several storage sheds—had to be repaired and painted, so there was plenty of work to be done, and everyone worked hard.

At the end of the week Glory felt a twinge of homesickness. She was busy, but even as she worked she found herself thinking of family. With Jared gone she felt unaccountably lonely, even though when he was there, she seldom saw him. On Thursday, as she was making arrangements to have Lucy flown to the estate the next day, she had a sudden inspiration. Jared had told her that any time she wanted to bring family to visit she was welcome to do so. He understood the disadvantages of working so far from civilization, and he was willing to compromise his own privacy just to keep his staff happy. Now, since he was gone, his privacy wouldn't suffer at all.

On impulse, Glory called her sister Peggy, who had taken over Glory's old job at the Aikane. Peggy had the weekend off and was delighted to be invited to visit, so Glory made arrangements for her to fly up from Lihue with Lucy.

It was with a flutter of excitement that Glory watched the helicopter land the next afternoon. Peggy was nineteen, and she and Glory were as different as sisters could be. But Peggy was family, and they had grown up to be close friends. Glory had missed her.

Peggy bounded out of the helicopter at the last turn of the blades. Peggy always bounded. She had enormous reserves of energy, and the more active she was, the happier. She dashed across the lawn and into Glory's arms for a bear hug that belied her petite frame. "Aloha *kaikuahine*! They've got you living in the middle of nowhere."

Glory laughed and hugged Peggy before pushing her back to look at her. "You've cut your hair!"

Peggy ruffled her mass of shoulder-length curls. "You know I couldn't stand all that hair. It was like a mop. Now at least I can get a brush through it."

"I'm glad I wasn't there to hear what Mama said, but I think you're gorgeous." And she was. Peggy's curls framed a face that, like her sister's, reflected their diverse heritage, but in different ways. Her skin was peach toned, and her dark hair had russet highlights. Most unusual were her eyes, a pale tawny brown that was almost gold.

Peggy shrugged. "Look who's talking. I had to wait until you were gone just to look at myself in the mirror."

"You're crazy." Glory looked beyond her sister and watched a tiny Chinese woman with a salt-and-pepper Buster Brown hairstyle being helped out of the helicopter. "I almost forgot about Lucy. I'd better go greet her. We haven't met face-to-face."

"She's neat. You'll like her."

A voice sounded from behind Glory. "I'd be happy to greet Lucy for you if you'd like."

Glory turned to see Paradox staring at Lucy, entranced. Glory was learning to appreciate the butler's subtle humor and kind heart. He was a paradox indeed, a large, shy man, strong enough to squash any foe, yet too sensitive to want to hurt even the occasional mouse that found its way inside. She had seen him trap the small creatures with a towel and his huge gentle hand and carry them outside to freedom. Glory had never had to ask how he'd gotten his nickname. "Do you know Lucy?" she asked, surprised at his offer.

"Yes. We went to school together when we were children."

Glory lowered her voice. "Why didn't you tell me?" Lucy was walking slowly toward them, and Glory had a feeling this was one conversation she shouldn't hear.

"I knew you'd hire her once you tasted her cooking."

"How would you know about her cooking?" She was whispering now.

"I always eat at the Beach Hut when I go down below." Paradox brushed gently by Glory, almost knocking her off her feet. "Lucy," he said, holding out one hand, "welcome to Wehilani."

"A romance," Glory said. "Right under my nose, and I didn't suspect."

Peggy laughed as she kicked Goblin with her heels to make him catch up to Ghost. "You were manipulated, that's for sure." She kicked once more, but Goblin just ambled along. *"Pa'akiki!"*

Glory smiled. Goblin *was* stubborn, but her rider was more so. "I thought the two of you would be a good match."

"And to think that one day last week I almost missed you. Course it turned out to be the flu instead."

Glory laughed at her sister. They'd had one lovely day together catching up on all they had missed. Now, on the last day before Peggy headed home, they were on a ride to explore more of the estate. Peggy was wearing rust-colored jeans and a lime-green sweatshirt with the sleeves chopped off. She had gathered half her hair on top of her head in a topknot, and the rest bounced around her face with every one of Goblin's jolting steps. She looked about ten.

"Paradox put one over on me," Glory admitted. "I can't figure out how much Lucy knew. One thing's for sure, though. If Paradox has his way, there'll be a wedding here before summer."

"Minamina," Peggy scoffed, using the Hawaiian expression for "too bad." "Just one?"

Glory turned back to the path in front of her. "Peggy..." she warned.

"Well, it seems like a fair question. You're obviously smitten with this Jared person."

"And you're obviously mistaken."

"Then you're saying, outright, honestly, forthrightly, that you're not falling in love?"

"I'm not saying anything."

"You've said enough already. I can put two and two together."

"Don't strain, Peg. Addition was never your subject."

"But trying to hide your feelings was always yours, wasn't it?"

They'd ridden in silence for a while before Glory spoke again. "Suppose, just for argument's sake, that you were right. Wouldn't that be the craziest thing in the world? Jared Farrell is *he kanaka ikaika*, as rich and powerful as one of the ancient *ali'i* who ruled this island. And me? Well, I'm just me. Not rich, not powerful. What would I have to offer him?"

Peggy was silent for a while, too, but when she spoke it was obvious she was angry. "You know what? You live in the middle of one of those legends of yours. You've never really been part of this century. I dance the hula and ride in the *pau* club and keep the old crafts alive because it's fun. When you're doing those things, you're wishing you'd lived three hundred years ago!"

Glory reined in her horse and dismounted. She didn't look at Peggy as she walked to a wall of rocks and pulled herself up on them to gaze into a small grove of trees. Even so, she knew when Peggy joined her.

"Ua kaumaha au," Peggy apologized, touching Glory's knee.

"I'm sorry, too. I wish you hadn't told the truth, because I really didn't want to hear it."

"I exaggerated. *Two* hundred years ago. At the most."

Glory laughed. She had never been able to stay mad at Peggy for long.

"Really, though, haven't you figured out by now that you have everything to offer? Where's this sudden inferiority complex coming from?" Peggy reached between the rocks and plucked a small white flower, dropping it in Glory's lap.

Glory took the flower and twisted it into her hair. "I know what I have to offer. I also know what Jared Farrell needs. The two—"

"What does he need?" Peggy asked, interrupting. "A Yale graduate? Someone whose ancestors sailed to Massachusetts on the Mayflower instead of paddling an outrigger canoe to the islands?"

"You're bound and determined to make me sound like I'm ashamed of who I am!"

"Aren't you? This is America, Kololia. Hawaii might have been a monarchy once, but there are no *ali'i* or *mo'i* now."

Glory was silent for a while, wondering how right Peggy was. "He's been hurt," she said finally. "He doesn't trust women. He was engaged last year to someone named Patsy Hightower. Supposedly I look like—"

"Patsy Hightower?" Peggy gave a low whistle. "Hot stuff."

"You know her?"

"Let's just say I've seen her." She drew out her next words. "All of her—or almost."

"Ha'i mai!" Glory demanded. She knew Peggy would drag the story out, and Glory was too intrigued to be patient. "Come on, tell me!"

"Jeff had this calendar, one of those Island Beauty of the Month numbers. Miss May was Patsy Hightower. I remember, because she looked so much like you that I did a double take at first. That's why I remember her name."

Glory was torn between trying to find out how her fourteen-year-old brother had managed to sneak the calendar past their mother and asking just what Patsy had been wearing.

Peggy answered the latter without being asked. "She was wearing a waterfall," Peggy said smugly. "And she's not as pretty as you are. And that's the woman who was almost good enough for Jared Farrell, king of Wehilani?"

"This is a crazy conversation."

Peggy shrugged. "It may be crazy, but I'd say knowing about Patsy Hightower's *he mea waiwai loa*. A very valuable thing," she repeated in English for emphasis.

Glory already had too much to absorb, not the least being Peggy's accusation that she didn't believe she was good enough for Jared. She was painfully aware of how close to the mark her sister had been. "I'm not ashamed of who I am," she said, sliding off the rock and dusting the back of her jeans. "But I guess I really have been intimidated by who Jared is."

"He's a *kane*. Just a man—a breed I thought you understood."

"I guess I thought I did, too." Glory smiled, then twirled around. "Well, how do I look?"

"Opulepule."

"Just kind of crazy?" Glory twirled again. "Don't you notice anything? Look! I'm off my pedestal, Peggy. Now you're giving *me* advice."

"Took me nineteen years to get up the courage." Peggy let out a shriek as Glory playfully charged her.

"Now you've had it." Glory started after Peggy, who was running like the wind. The game was an old one. Both knew it would end when they collapsed with laughter.

Peggy darted between the rocks where they had been sitting and Glory followed, cutting through a patch of trees to head her off. Peggy wheeled just as Glory reached her and started toward a break in the cliff that lay behind the trees.

"Malama pono," Glory called in warning as she slowed to a walk. When Peggy kept running, she called again, louder, "Be careful, Peg. Don't fall off the mountain."

Peggy stopped at the gap in the cliff, but she didn't turn back. She edged forward, her back to the rocks so that she could slide between.

Glory's heart lodged in her throat. To her knowledge, the only thing that could be beyond the rocks was air. She hadn't explored this area with Jared, and she and Peggy were well off the flight path of Jared's helicopter or the sight-seeing helicopters that roamed the Kauai skies. They were bordering state land. Peggy was either about to walk in space or drop straight down into a valley owned by the honorable people of Hawaii.

She opened her mouth to call another warning when Peggy turned and motioned her to be silent. Glory frowned as her sister disappeared. She had little choice except to follow.

The crack in the cliff wall was narrow enough that she had to move slowly, inching along. She was about to give up on ever seeing Peggy again when she came to an opening. Peggy was crouching there, peering through another crack in the rocks that made the one Glory had just come through seem as large as nearby Waimea Canyon.

"What on earth—" Glory quieted as Peggy shook her head in warning. Then she followed Peggy's beckoning hand and went to crouch beside her.

Peggy moved sideways so that Glory could see. Just beyond them was neither empty space nor state land. It was a sheltered valley, hidden by the mountains on three sides and a thick grove of trees on the fourth. Glory knew it belonged to Wehilani by the familiar yellow markers that posted the borders of Jared's land.

Not all the markers were in place, however. Some of them had been incorporated into the four crudely constructed huts that sat in a circle at the edge of the forest. As Glory stared, she saw two men, large muscular Hawaiians, move out from behind the huts toward a familiar looking green patch growing beside a stream that ran down from the mountain above it. For a moment she was filled with horror. She knew what kind of crops were grown in secret locations like this one, and she knew what sometimes happened to the people who discovered them. Then common sense took control. She shaded her eyes to focus more intently.

"A taro patch," she whispered to Peggy.

"And a vegetable garden," Peggy whispered back. "Corn, beans, tomatoes. They've put in fruit trees, too." She pointed toward the right. "And check out the goats."

Glory saw that Peggy was right. There were goats in a pen beyond the taro patch. There were also native chickens, which curiously enough were a protected species on the island. As she watched, a small child barely old enough to toddle came from one of the huts to chase after a proud old rooster who ran, squawking furiously, toward the goat pen.

"How did you know this was here?" Glory asked just loudly enough for Peggy to hear.

"I didn't. But I thought I heard a shout. I was just snooping. What are they doing here?" Peggy stooped above Glory so that she could see, too.

"That looks fairly straightforward. They're homesteading."

"What a crazy place to own property!"

"Not crazy if it's part of a huge estate."

"You mean it's part of Wehilani?"

Glory sat back, propping herself against the rock. "That's exactly what I mean." She shut her eyes, but she could still see the huts, the garden, the goats. "They're trespassers."

Peggy slid down beside her. They were still talking in whispers. *"No ke aha?"*

"Why?" was a question Glory couldn't answer. She wished she knew. Another one just as important came to mind. "What am I going to do?"

"What do you mean?"

"What am I going to do? If I report them to Jared, the police will come and arrest them, destroy their homes."

"They're trespassers."

"They have a *keiki*. Did you see him? A beautiful little boy."

"I saw. He looks like he's about Nicky's age."

"There's no land to be bought on this island." Glory stared at the crack in the rocks through which they had come. "Not unless you're *waiwai*." She turned her hand palm up and rubbed her thumb across her fingertips to emphasize her point.

"They certainly aren't *waiwai*," Peggy conceded. "They wouldn't be living there if they had *any* money."

"They aren't hurting anybody."

"They could hurt *you* if the king of Wehilani finds out about them and suspects you knew."

"And Jared *will* find out." Glory stood and, without another look toward the small settlement in the valley, started back through the narrow canyon.

Peggy followed closely behind. "The miracle is that no one's seen them before this."

"Someone will. They're off the major flight path, and they're sheltered. But someone will fly over and notice them. It's just a matter of time."

"Then maybe you should be the one to tell Jared. You could throw yourself on him and beg for mercy."

Glory knew her sister well enough to know that Peggy joked when she was most moved. She was silent as she finished her crab walk through the narrow canyon. Ghost and Goblin were grazing happily when the two women approached.

Glory didn't mount right away. She stroked Ghost's neck, deep in thought.

"Kololia?" Peggy asked at last.

"You were only seven when our father died. How much do you remember about that time?"

"As little as possible."

"Do you remember living with Aunt Pua?"

"I'm afraid so."

Glory turned and faced her sister. "There were twelve of us, Peg, in a house meant for four. We lived that way for a year because we had no place else to go. And we were lucky we had that. If we hadn't had relatives to go to, we would have been homeless. Because of them, Mama was able to work and save so she could afford a place for us."

"You don't know these people are in that situation," Peggy protested.

Glory shook her head sadly. "Could a man with everything understand people with nothing?"

Peggy just shrugged as they mounted and turned the horses back toward the house.

They were a good distance from the village in the valley before Glory spoke again.

"If I tell Jared, I'll be responsible for bringing those people *pilikia*." Then she thought of the *pilikia*—trouble—that she might get in if Jared discovered she had found the village and not reported it, and she released a long ragged breath.

Peggy was obviously thinking of all the implications of Glory's decision. "If you don't tell, what else will you do to protect them? Will you keep people from this part of the estate? Will you make sure there aren't any flights to check the property?"

"No, I can't interfere or lie for them."

"I don't know what I'd do if I were you," Peggy admitted.

Glory didn't tell her sister that, as they'd ridden, she had made one decision. She was going to wait a week or two, and then she was going to go back and see if the homesteaders were still there. If they were, she was going to talk to them. She knew Peggy would tell her not to take that kind of risk and the advice would be correct. Unfortunately, it was advice she couldn't follow. She had to know more.

It was late afternoon when they arrived back at the house. Lucy and Paradox were sitting together on the east wing lanai. From a distance, Glory could see that they were deep in conversation. As she and Peggy rode into the stable yard, Sally and Rolfe strolled by. Glory seldom saw the long-married couple together, but now she noted they were holding hands. One Leg was camping again, with a "lady friend of long acquaintance" as Sally had put it that morning, raising her eyebrows suggestively. It seemed as if everyone at Wehilani had someone, everyone except Glory and Jared.

Now, with the secret of the homesteaders lying heavily between them, Glory knew that she and Jared were being pulled further apart. In a way the homesteaders symbolized all their problems. And her inability to talk to him about them was the most important problem of all.

"It's so quiet here," Peggy said as she dismounted to begin unsaddling Goblin.

Glory knew the statement wasn't a compliment. Vivacious Peggy, who needed to be doing three things at once, wouldn't be happy living at Wehilani.

For the first time since Glory had come, she wondered if she could continue to be happy here herself.

Chapter Seven

Going off for the whole day?" One Leg nudged Ghost's saddle into place and bent to fasten the girth.

Glory finished braiding a spray of vanda orchids into the mare's silver mane, then stood back to admire the effect. "I wish I could, but I've got some paperwork to finish this afternoon."

"A fine young lady like yourself shouldn't be spending so much time cooped up in an office."

Glory smiled. One Leg was a noble flatterer and just about old enough to be her grandfather. Like the rest of the staff, he had more than accepted her—he had taken her under his wing. A man with a sly sense of humor, he was prone to giving advice and telling outrageous stories about his days in the Australian outback. Glory enjoyed one as much as the other and discounted both.

"Well, I won't be cooped up this morning." She lifted Ghost's bridle over her head and came around to the horse's side, slinging the canvas bag with her art supplies over the saddle horn.

"Seems a shame, Miss Glorious, to waste those flash clothes on Ghost."

Glory laughed as she mounted. "They aren't wasted, One Leg. You've seen me. I've seen me."

"The two of you look like you're in a blooming parade."

"A *blooming* parade?" Glory fingered her multicolored lei, holding it away from her chest. "Blooming?"

He chortled appreciatively. "You're lucky. *My* sister sends presents, too. Last month I got socks she'd made out of wool she'd carded herself. Still had sticks and briars in it!"

Glory pulled an orange hibiscus from behind her ear and bent to tuck it behind One Leg's. She wasn't sure, but she thought he blushed. "Aloha."

"Mahalo." He slapped Ghost on the rump. "And aloha to you."

Glory blinked as she and Ghost emerged into bright sunshine. It was one of Wehilani's rare golden days. The Hawaiian language had thirty-three ways to describe a cloud, and in her days here on the mountain, Glory thought she'd seen all those types and more besides. But today, as if they'd signed a temporary treaty, what clouds there were drifted by in filmy cobweb patches that couldn't hide the sky.

She wasn't sure if it was the sunlight bathing the breathtaking countryside or Peggy's gift that had made her decide to take the morning off. The gift had come by way of Dave, who had flown up the week's provisions. Glory had opened a long florist's box to discover two multicolored leis and an array of lovely single blossoms. The enclosed note had simply said: *"A hui hou kakou."* Until we meet again.

Whichever it was, the sunshine or Peggy's gift, Glory had awakened that morning determined to set aside Glory: Wehilani manager, and become Glory: dreamer, writer, artist. In that mood, she had gone to her closet for jeans and pulled out her *pau* rider's costume instead. Bringing it all had been a whim. It was too delicate for hard riding, too peacock bright for anything except special occasions. But somehow it had ended up in her luggage, and after no thought at all, this morning it had ended up on her slender body.

Now, thinking about it, she realized that the real reason she'd worn the costume today was to cheer herself up.

For the past week the homesteaders had weighed heavily on her mind. She hadn't made a decision about whether to tell Jared, but she had thought a great deal about what might happen if he discovered the village first and asked if she had known it was there.

Of course, it was possible he wouldn't ask. If no one else had noticed it thus far, he probably wouldn't even consider that she might have. Despite that probability, she'd already decided she would tell him that she'd known about the villagers, because if what she suspected was true, she would be forced to plead their cause.

She hadn't been back to confirm her suspicions, but Glory knew in her heart that the people in the hidden valley were there because they had no other place to go. Like Koolau the leper, they were living off the goodness of the land because they had no choice. They were paying the price for being poor in paradise.

Jared would understand suffering. Because of what Sally had told her, Glory knew he had suffered, too. But Jared wouldn't understand what it meant to be so poor that desperate acts seemed the only solution. The homeless in cities had to depend on doorways to shelter them and soup kitchens to feed them. But here, even though there were miles of fertile land with nature's bounty waiting to be harvested, the suffering could be as great—because that fertile land belonged to someone else.

Wehilani belonged to Jared, as it had belonged to other Farrells before him. But before the Farrells, the land had belonged to people like those homesteading in the secret valley. Now those people could not afford the land that their ancestors had once sold so cheaply. Would Jared understand their plight? Would he understand their pain and reach out to help them, or would he prosecute, using the law to keep untainted what was legally his?

She remembered the disdain in his voice when he had talked about Wehilani becoming a resort community. She remembered that he had bought the entire point on Poipu Beach to keep it from becoming a hotel. And she remembered his reaction to the campers. He was a man who valued privacy above all else. The homesteaders had breached that privacy. She was sure she knew what his response would be.

She wasn't afraid of losing her job; she knew she could find another one. She wasn't afraid of standing up for what she believed in; she had been taught never to take the easy way out. Her feelings went deeper than fear. She had few illusions that Jared would ever return the love she was beginning to feel for him. But, even if the impossible were to happen, the secret of the homesteaders stood between them now, a barrier that seemed insurmountable.

With an impatient shake of her head, she tried to put the villagers and Jared out of her mind. There was nothing she could do about either, now. She had decided to take the morning off so she could forget everything and concentrate on her book. She wanted to make use of this perfect day without the worry that had dogged every minute of the past week.

Taking One Leg's advice, she rode toward the waterfall on the path behind the stables. One Leg had told her of a fork she could take so that she didn't have to hike in for the last hundred yards or so. The path wound over a ridge and through a densely wooded forest festooned with shiny-leafed yam vines. After thirty minutes of wondering if she had understood the directions, she heard the song of water moving swiftly over rocks.

Ghost moved faster, as if she knew that arriving at the falls meant a long rest and all the greenery she could nibble. Glory stopped and dismounted once, in the midst of a lush flowering meadow. She fingered but didn't pick the scarlet feathery flowers blooming on scrubby bushes beside the path. The flowers weren't the only attraction. A straggling vine with shiny oval leaves grew there, too. She smiled triumphantly at the sight, picking handfuls of long shoots to tuck into her canvas bag of supplies.

She reached the turnoff to the waterfall after a short ride. It was as lovely as she had imagined, a small falls of perhaps ten feet that fell into a clear rocky pool before the water seeped into a channel and continued as a placid stream.

Ghost whinnied as if to tell Glory she was on her own now.

"Ho'omalimali," she scolded softly, stroking the horse's neck as she asked her for patience. "Can't you take me farther?" She slackened the reins, and Ghost did just that, stopping beside the falls. Glory slid down, taking her bag of supplies with her. She stroked the horse's nose in thanks before she dropped the reins to free her.

She had reached heaven. If the Hawaiian Islands were paradise, then she had ascended one step farther. Nothing and nowhere could be more breathtaking than this spot. The waterfall sparkled in the sunlight, each crystal droplet a diamond of matchless splendor that merged into a fine rainbow spray. The full spectrum of colors danced against rocks that were a glistening pewter.

The rocky pool was surrounded by lush ferns living harmoniously with vines and low-lying shrubs. There was a cave behind it, carved by water and time into a fern-lined hollow. The water falling in a delicate veil across its opening seemed to whisper, "Come, explore. *Ma'i maka'u.* Don't be afraid."

Ghost wandered off, less impressed by nature's masterwork than by the promise of grass just beyond the rocks. Glory drew in a deep breath and inhaled the perfume of life: clean air and dark, rich soil; rain transformed into waterfalls; the living green of plants and the subtle scent of flowers.

She wasn't sure how long she stood that way, drawing in the essence of this secret place. She heard the call of birds and felt a warm breeze caress her skin. Finally, with a sigh of pleasure, she walked to a flat rock near the falls, but not so near that she would get wet, and sat down to spread her supplies in front of her.

Jared found her there an hour later. The sound of his arrival had been hidden by the music of the falls. He stopped at the turnoff and dismounted, leaving Demon to join Ghost, who was grazing contentedly. He couldn't pull his gaze from the brightest blossom he had seen on his ride: Glory, dressed in a split skirt of orange-and-salmon swirls and a white blouse with a high neck and long puffed sleeves. Around her neck were two leis, and on her hair, which was piled high on her head, was a wreath or *hei* of tiny white flowers.

He had never seen anything as lovely. All her attention was concentrated on a tablet in front of her, and she was as still as an artist's model.

He walked toward her slowly, and so deep was her concentration that she didn't look up until his shadow fell across the tablet.

"Oh, Jared." For a moment she felt as if she had brought this proud, unsmiling man to life. Her eyes fell to the charcoal sketch she had been making, and she saw the man who stood in front of her. But the man in front of her was dressed in dark jeans and a white shirt rolled up at the elbows. The man in her drawing was dressed as a warrior in a feather cloak and brown tapa cloth.

When she looked up again, she saw that Jared was trying to examine the drawing. Slowly, as if it meant nothing, she lifted the tablet and closed it, bending to put it into the canvas bag.

She straightened and stood. "I didn't know you were coming back today. We were expecting you on Monday."

He went through the motions of answering as his gaze wandered over her, feasting on every feature. "My meetings ended sooner than I'd expected. I caught a flight out of Detroit last night with two minutes to spare. I didn't have a chance to let anyone know."

"You must be very tired." She could see fine lines of fatigue etched around his eyes, and she was surprised that he had come to the falls to find her instead of going straight to bed.

He caught her gaze and held it. "I slept on the flight. I'm all right."

She didn't know what else to say. His unwavering stare was so intense it seemed to burn right through her. She felt its heat like two glowing coals.

He moved closer, and the heat seemed to ignite the air between them. "I've thought about you. The whole time I've been away, I've thought of nothing but you."

She shut her eyes, but the heat still blazed between them. "Jared..." Her throat was dry, and she swallowed. She felt his hands on her cheeks; they seemed to singe her skin.

"Tell me you haven't thought of me, too."

She wanted to answer that she hadn't thought of him. Visions of the tiny unsanctioned village flickered through her head, and she imagined she could see Jared's fury when he found that she had kept it secret.

She opened her eyes to tell him that he was mistaken, that she thought of him as nothing but the man she worked for. The words wouldn't come.

Jared read her true answer. With a groan he pulled her close and covered her mouth with his. She pressed against him, her body unconsciously seeking the heat of his. She felt as if he were devouring her, and she fed his hunger, moving her lips under his, seeking, demanding.

Nothing had ever felt so right. Nothing had ever been so wrong. Some sane part of her remembered the problems between them; some irrational part of her didn't care. She drew in his essence, just as she'd absorbed the essence of this secret place. His scent was male and vital; his skin was hot. She listened to the harsh sound of his breathing and savored the sweet-salty taste of him against her lips. She wondered what satanic forces had brought them together so that the truth could tear them apart.

His hands moved from her back to her waist, recklessly seeking more. He pressed her tighter against him, and she felt her body melt into his. He wanted her in the most primal of ways, and, even knowing that, she still couldn't make herself pull away.

His lips left hers to travel restlessly across her cheeks. "I've wanted to kiss you. Forever."

"Jared..." She didn't know what else to say. She didn't have the strength to turn him away. She had tried so hard not to imagine herself in his arms. She had told herself that she could never be anything to him. Now she realized how she had lied. Nothing was real except this.

She felt the rasp of his cheek as his lips tormented her earlobe. His breath against her sensitized skin was tantalizing fire, and she moaned in response.

His laughter was husky. Possessive. His hands traced her spine, lingering at her neck and, finally, found their way into her hair. He pulled out the pins as he spoke, until it was a black cloak covering her back. "The night we stayed at the beach house, I didn't sleep. I imagined you lying there, a room away, and I wondered what you would say, what you would do, if I came to you."

"I would have yearned to say yes." She gasped as he kissed her again, bending her in his arms until she knew how hard it would be to say no to him now.

"Glory. *Healoha.*"

Tears sprang to her eyes. He had used the Hawaiian word for "loved one." She felt her own love grow inside her, smothering all her fears, all her resistance. She knew at that moment that he had captured her heart, and that it would be his forever.

He kissed her again, but he forced himself to make the kiss gentler. He was desperately close to asking for more than she was prepared to give, and he knew that if he didn't pull back now, he would soon be too desperate to know better. Never in all his years had he wanted a woman the way he wanted Glory.

With a ragged sigh he wove his hands into her hair, lifted it and let it fall through his fingers. "You are so beautiful," he whispered against her cheek. "If Kauai were a woman, she would look like you."

She trembled against him, so filled with feeling that it spilled over into her words. "Jared, I've dreamed of this, but I've told myself some dreams can never come true."

"I've dreamed, too." He tucked her head against his shoulder and held her close. Glory could feel him fight for control. There was a battle raging inside him: caution warring with a flood tide of feeling. As he fought himself, she fought for composure, too. There was a chasm between them, deep and wide and filled with silent lies. He wasn't a man who would give his trust easily, and if he gave it to her, it would be undeserved.

Still, she couldn't tell him about the homesteaders. Not until she knew more.

A minute went by before he slowly began to release her, struggling as he did so with the part of him that wanted so much more. "Show me your drawings," he said softly, the words squeezed from a throat taut with desire.

The request was so unexpected that for a moment she couldn't answer. "I... you don't have to pretend to be interested," she said at last. "It's only a hobby."

"I am interested."

His arms dropped to his side. Then, because he couldn't yet bear the parting, he lifted his hands to her face, framing it and raising it to his. "I find I'm interested in everything about you."

She smiled a little, but she felt very close to tears. "Perhaps you shouldn't be."

"Why not?"

"Perhaps what you find might not be enough to hold your interest."

He smiled, too, and for a moment a look of indescribable tenderness softened his face. "Perhaps what I find might hold my interest forever."

Her eyes dropped as tears stung them.

"Will you show me the drawings?" he asked, forcing his hands to his sides once more.

She didn't know how to refuse. "Yes." She turned without looking at him again and lowered herself to the rock. Jared sat beside her, although he didn't trust himself to sit close enough to touch her again, and waited.

Her hands were trembling as she pulled the tablet from the bag. "These are just sketches," she said. It took considerable effort to flip back the cardboard cover of the tablet and reveal the first drawing.

He had asked to see the sketches as a way to put distance between them. He was interested in everything about Glory, but until she revealed the first drawing, he'd had no idea that what he'd asked to see would be a series of small masterpieces.

The sketch was of a Hawaiian woman. She was middle-aged and overweight, but she had a queenly presence, with head held high and back straight, even though it was apparent that she was exhausted. She was standing on the shore, waves lapping at her feet, and she gazed wistfully out to sea as if an answer to life's problems could be found there. One arm was outstretched as if in a voiceless plea to the faint rainbow over her head.

Jared was stunned by the power of the drawing. He had only glimpsed the page Glory had been working on when he first found her. Now this drawing leaped out at him as if the woman's life, her dreams, her fears, had been documented by Glory's skillful fingers.

Glory waited. She risked one glance at Jared's face, but she could read nothing there. With the desire to get this torture over quickly, she turned the page.

The second drawing was of the same woman, back bent under the weight of a heavy fishing net. She turned the page again, and the woman reappeared, weary beyond endurance, her head in her hands.

"There's a story here," Jared said, beginning to see that the drawings were a sequence.

"It's one of our legends. The story of Lono Moku, the woman in the moon. Do you know it?"

Jared shook his head. When Glory didn't turn the page, he covered her hand and did it for her. The next picture showed the woman bathed in the wondrous light of a rainbow.

Softly she told the story as she followed his lead and continued to turn the pages. "Once Lono Moku was known as Hina. She lived with her husband by the sea. He was a bad-tempered, lazy man who required her to do all the work while he slept in the sunshine. Her children were all gone, and each year she became wearier."

"One afternoon, after she had worked hard since sunrise, her husband demanded that she take a net down to the sea and catch some shrimp for his dinner. She was so tired that when she stood on the shore, she began to wish out loud that the waves would carry her away in their warm embrace." Glory turned back to the first sketch, which showed that moment. Then she went on.

"The rainbow spanning the sky above her head heard her wish and, taking pity on her, began to unroll itself until one end lay on the waves at her feet. The rainbow told her that it had heard her plea and knew her sadness. It offered itself as a ladder into the bright blue sky, but warned Hina that it could not say what she might find there."

Glory turned the page and showed Hina beginning her journey. "Hina knew that nothing but unhappiness awaited her on earth, so she began to climb." She flipped to the next page. "She climbed and climbed, but the closer she came to the sun, the harder was each step she took. She was still holding the net, and she used it as shelter, over her head, but nothing could shield her from the sun's rays. The closer she came, the more pain she suffered, until she lost consciousness and fell to the earth."

Jared took in the sketch that showed Hina falling. Glory had exactly portrayed her fright, her sense of defeat, her pain.

"When Hina fell back to earth, it was nighttime. Without the sun's rays to burn away all her strength, she began to recover. As she lay on the beach she saw her husband come by with a calabash full of fresh water that he had dipped from the spring. He raved at her for being a bad wife and disappearing for the afternoon."

Glory hadn't portrayed the husband. Only his feet were shown beside Hina's weary head, which still lay in the sand. One foot was lifted angrily, as if to kick her.

"Hina knew then that she must try to escape again. She went into the house and took her calabash, which had every possession she held dear inside it, and went back down to the sea. The rainbow was still there, soft and graceful in the moonlight. Hina began to climb toward the moon."

Glory had captured a mixture of expectation, unutterable fatigue and fear on Hina's face. Jared could not understand how she had done it with such a sparsity of line. The drawing was simple, and yet it was anything but. "Tell me she made it," he said at last, caught up in the story.

Glory was so surprised he had spoken that for a moment she forgot where she had left off. She risked another glance at his face and saw a frown of concentration.

"She made it, but with difficulty." Glory turned the page. "Her husband realized that she was leaving him. With Hina gone, there would be no one to wait on him. He would have to fend for himself. So he followed her. She had almost escaped him when he made one last leap and grabbed her foot, twisting it and injuring it before he fell back to earth. Hina continued on, lame and in pain, until she reached the moon, where she was welcomed and given a home."

Glory turned the page once more. This sketch showed a full moon shining against a palm-lined beach. "If you look up at the moon, you can see Hina," she said. "She sits there, her foot still lame, her calabash by her side. She is no longer called 'Hina,' but 'Lame Lono' or 'Lono Moku.' Sometimes she beats out tapa cloth, and the fine, soft clouds we see around the moon at night are really fine cloths she has made." She began to close the sketchbook, but he stopped her by covering her hands. His long fingers entwined with hers.

"Who was the woman you used as your model?"

"My mother." She raised her eyes to his and smiled a little, but he could feel the faint tremor in her hands. "She told us the story as children. We would go to the beach closest to our house and look up at the moon as she told it. She was often weary. Like Lono Moku, she had too much to do and too little help. I've always liked to picture her when I've thought of the lady in the moon, contented, rested at last."

"I'd like to meet your mother." Jared had told himself that he wouldn't kiss her again. They were too alone, and he wanted her too much. But words were only words. He bent toward her and brushed her lips with his. She tasted like a dream, and he knew that she would feel that way in his arms again, if he reached out for her. "You are immensely talented," he said huskily. "I'm awed."

For a moment she wasn't certain she had heard him correctly. He had said nothing about her sketches as he'd looked at them. She'd believed he hadn't been impressed. "Do you think so?"

Jared saw the doubt in her eyes, the tiny flicker of hope. He groaned and, defeated by temptation, pulled her into his arms again. "Glory, don't you know? How can you not know?"

The sketchbook was caught between them. Glory held on to Jared, afraid he was going to let her go. She lifted her chin and sought his mouth with hers. This time her lips opened willingly, and she felt the penetration of his tongue. She sensed the new intimacy in every part of her body, heat rising to suffuse and pulse through her until it burned away all thought.

She had never known what it was to burn before. Her body felt as if it belonged to someone else, so unfamiliar was each new sensation. She tilted her head and passionately met his tongue with hers, letting him guide her to greater pleasure. She felt his fingers digging into her back and her breasts pressing into his rock-hard chest. The only difference between them that seemed important were the ones that made this moment so achingly perfect.

Jared felt her wholehearted response even as he knew that it was new for her. She was unconsciously sensual, in tune with the rhythms and needs of her body, but she was inexperienced. She gave and she took with a sweet innocence that told him how new this kind of passion was for her.

She held nothing back, and Jared knew that if she wasn't to have her first lover here, on the flat rocks beside a waterfall, he would have to be the one to stop them again. She was too unschooled to know how quickly they were moving toward lovemaking.

He pulled his mouth from hers, trailing his lips along her jawline in a series of farewell kisses. She murmured her distress, and he kissed her lips once more, lingering for just a moment to drink their sweetness before he turned her head to his chest.

Glory could hear the trip-hammer beat of Jared's heart and feel the fine trembling in the hands that stroked her back. She felt as if she were fighting her way out of a trance toward a reality she didn't want. If the ecstasy of their kisses had been illusory, then reality was too harsh to bear.

"We're too good together, *healoha*," he cautioned. "And I want you too much."

She knew he was right, but she wished he was wrong. There had been nothing in her experience with other men to teach her the pleasure a man and a woman can bring each other.

When they finally parted, the sketchbook fell open. Glory looked down to see Jared's face—a warrior's face—staring up at her.

Jared saw it, too. Before she could close the book, he grasped it and held it up to study it. "And who is this?" he asked at last.

"That's Hakuole." She couldn't meet his eyes. She looked away.

"And does he have a story, too?"

"You must be tired of stories, Jared."

"Tell me."

"It's a story for women."

He touched her cheek, turning her face to his. "A lov story?"

Her nod was so slight that he had to guess she had give it.

"Tell me."

There were too many emotions in Jared's eyes for Glor to read them all. She looked away again, afraid he would se the same in hers.

She told the story with no adornment. "Hakuole was warrior loyal to King Kalanikupule. When Kamehameh came to conquer Oahu, Hakuole fought in the last battl But before that battle, while he was resting, he dreamed tha Leilehua, the daughter of the island priest, or *kahuna*, cam to him and dropped a lei of lehua flowers at his feet. Whe he sat up, the lei was there, in the doorway, but Leilehua wa not. Hakuole didn't care. He had seen the light of love in he eyes, and he knew that she would be his after the battle."

Jared began to turn the page to search for more sketche but Glory took it from his hands and held it to her breast.

His mouth twisted in a half smile. "Is that all? Surel there's more to the story."

"There's more," she said, guarding the book. "Hakuol and the warriors of King Kalanikupule weren't successfu Kamehameha took the island of Oahu, uniting the eight i lands. Those who survived, including the *kahuna* father (Leilehua, brought gifts to the new king. In fact the *k huna*'s gift *was* Leilehua. She knelt weeping before the ne king when a man, bloodied and torn from battle, strode int the circle around Kamehameha. It was Hakuole, still wea ing his lei of lehua blossoms. He lifted Leilehua off th ground and carried her away."

"And Kamehameha let him?"

"No, the guards swiftly brought the young couple bac Everyone present waited for Kamehameha to sentence th young man to a terrible death, but instead, because (Hakuole's courage, the king gave him Leilehua. To Leil hua he gave all the lands that had once been her father's. Then he told them both that their love should be as glorious to Hawaii as the wars of Kamehameha. And with his words, he forever sealed the love of the people of the islands for their new king."

Jared rested his hands lightly on Glory's shoulders, then, inch by inch, slid them slowly to the top of her breasts, which were blocked by the sketch pad. "I'd like to see Leilehua. Is she as beautiful as the blossom from which she gets her name?"

"I'm not satisfied with her."

"Aren't you?" His hands tightened on the book. "Maybe I should help you judge?"

"Jared..." She dropped her hands to her side, refusing to engage in a tug of war. His hands lingered as the back of his fingers caressed the cloth-covered flesh behind the sketch pad. Then he drew the pad toward him and flipped it open once again. He came to the sketch of Hakuole, whose face he had recognized as the same one that gazed back from his mirror every morning. Slowly he turned to the next page.

Entwined with Hakuole, her face alight with love and her body worshipping his, was Leilehua.

Her face was familiar, too.

Jared could hardly breathe. He stared at the innocently erotic drawing for a long moment, then closed the sketchbook, tucking it back into the bag. But even without the drawing in front of him, the vision of his arms and legs wrapped around Glory's flower-adorned body was crystal clear in his imagination. He took longer to close the canvas flaps than he had to, restraining himself to keep from bringing the drawing to life here on the rocks. When he finally sat up, Glory's smooth tan skin was tinted an attractive rose.

"You put your dreams and the dreams of the Hawaiian people on paper," he said carefully, lifting her chin gently so that their eyes were level. "Why?"

"A children's book. Someday, when I'm satisfied with what I've done, I want to try and have it published."

"You're ready now."

Her eyes didn't quite meet his. "Do you think so?"

"Every sketch is perfect. Except possibly that last one. No child would understand it." He paused until she looked at him. "*I* understand it."

"Once times were simpler," she said sadly.

"I don't think Hakuole and Leilehua were caught in simple times, *healoha*."

She caught her breath as he kissed her. Then, just as she succumbed to the temptation of his lips again, he pulled away. "I have something for you."

She watched him stride away toward the small grassy clearing where Ghost and Demon had wandered. He disappeared behind jutting rocks, then reappeared a minute later, his hands full of flowers.

She recognized the scarlet flowers of the meadow she had passed through to reach the falls. "Lehua," she said, giving in to a shy smile.

"And I didn't know the story," he reminded her.

Abruptly her smile widened. "They're so lovely."

Jared sat down beside her, heaping the flowers in her lap.

"There's another story you don't know," she warned. She shook her head at the question in his eyes. "You'll know it soon enough." She reached inside the canvas bag, past the sketchbook, and lifted out the vines that she had picked in the meadow.

"Maile," she said, holding it out for him to smell. "As it dries it becomes more fragrant. I was going to weave it into Ghost's mane." Deftly she began to braid the shoots together. "This was the favorite lei of old Hawaii," she explained as she worked, her hands flying quickly over the vine. "It's spoken of in many of our ancient chants."

The lei grew as Jared watched. Her hands were as graceful as a tree dancing in a summer breeze. He wasn't a man given to patience, but he could have sat there forever and watched her work. Next to holding her in his arms, it was the greatest of pleasures.

When she had finished, the lei was about two-and-a-half feet long. She didn't fasten it into a circle, but left it in the traditional form, open at the ends. Then she chose the best blossoms from the feathery red lehua in her lap and wove them into the lei. When she was finished she frowned.

"It's not long enough." She brightened. "It doesn't matter, does it?"

He had trouble answering. He was still caught in the spell of her graceful flying fingers. He bent toward her, and she placed the lei around his neck. "Aloha," she said softly. "*Healoha.*"

The lei was crushed between them as he showed her in the only way he knew what she was coming to mean to him.

Finally he pulled away, his self-control dangling by threads. "It's time to go."

Glory didn't have to ask why. She knew that if they stayed in this tiny bit of heaven he would teach her more about heaven than she had ever hoped to learn. She also knew that the time wasn't right for that, and might never be.

She gave him her hand, and they walked slowly to the grassy clearing to mount Ghost and Demon. Glory's cheeks were flushed and her lips swollen from Jared's kisses. He could barely look at her sensually charged beauty.

He cast around for something, anything, to divert his attention. "There was another story," he reminded her as they mounted. "Or did you forget to tell me?"

She laughed softly. "I told you that you'd know soon enough."

"And what will I know?"

Glory rode Ghost to his side, then, with new boldness, she leaned over to kiss Jared's cheek. He met her halfway, turning his face to hers so that the kiss became a wonderful thing. She drew away as Ghost danced beneath her, anxious to be on the way home.

"Ghost knows," she said mysteriously.

"Ghost knows what?"

"It's going to rain."

Jared frowned up at the sky. The cobweb clouds that had previously drifted lazily by were gathering as if in an outraged summit meeting. "It'll pass over." He turned back to Glory. Her smile was wide. "You don't believe me, do you?"

"If you pick lehua as you're going somewhere, it will rain. If you pick it on the way home, the sun will still shine. That's why I didn't pick any when I got the maile. Unfortunately, you did."

"A superstition, not a story."

"And you're an unbeliever, not a man of faith." She kicked Ghost gently, starting along the trail. "An unbeliever who will soon be wet."

In a moment she heard Jared and Demon trotting behind her.

Thunder rumbled in the mountains as they passed through the lehua meadow. The scarlet blossoms danced in the restless wind to the music of the first raindrops and Jared's laughter.

Chapter Eight

Glory looked up from her desk and saw Jared lounging in the doorway, watching her. There was no smile on his face. His expression was feral, a famished beast spotting the prey he'd stalked for most of a week.

Now, six days after their morning at the waterfall, she found that it only took one such look, one brush of Jared's body as she passed him in the hall, one stolen kiss in the moonlight, and the very core of her turned hot and liquid.

They would be lovers soon. All it would take was for one of them to breach the thin veneer of control that had kept them apart this long. All it would take was one breathless yes.

Glory didn't know what Jared's control was made of. Fear, perhaps. Distrust. Experiences that told him women wanted him for the wrong reasons. Experiences that told him women often were *not* what they seemed.

Her control was made of sorrow. She was not what she seemed, not what she wanted to be. She held a lie closely guarded inside her. But no matter how often she had tried to reason that the lie was worse than the consequences of the truth, she had not been able to tell Jared about the homesteaders.

"What are you working on?"

Jared's deep voice could reach inside Glory and wring her emotions until she lost every trace of judgment and objectivity. Serenity, which had once been the cloak that she could hide behind, seemed gone forever.

She tried to sound businesslike—she was afraid she only sounded dazed. "I'm getting the household accounts together so that we can send them down to your accountant."

"I'm flying down to the beach house this afternoon. Would you like to join me?"

The question and the possibility twanged along her nerve endings. She wondered if he was asking for more than a day in the sun. She wondered how long it would be before she could no longer fight that possibility.

"We'll be chaperoned," he said as if in answer to her silent question. "I have a business acquaintance and his wife coming in from the Big Island. I thought you could help me entertain them."

She longed to say yes, but she had been waiting for Jared to leave Wehilani so that she could ride back to the village and talk to the homesteaders without being questioned about where she was going. She couldn't tell him a lie, even if by *not* telling him the truth she was already being dishonest.

"I can't go," she said. "I've got some other things I have to do that just can't wait. I'm sorry."

Jared wasn't a man to insist or pry. He wanted to know what was more important than sharing a day with him, but his pride kept him from asking. "All right."

He didn't move. His tall lean body filled the doorway, and, if possible, the indolent posture made him more attractive. He smiled slowly, as a wolf might smile if it could, just as it reached out for its quarry. "Come here, Glory."

She wondered if he was going to use his exquisite lovemaking to change her mind. She wanted to refuse to go to him, but she was already on her feet before it occurred to her.

She stopped an arm's length away. "Are you going to coerce me?" she asked as lightly as she could.

"Would it work?"

"I won't tell."

"Shall we experiment?"

She shook her head.

He reached out with lightning speed and gripped her shoulder, spinning her into his embrace. "You'd distract me, anyway. I can't think about anyone else when you're near." He punctuated his words with a long slow kiss that left them both out of breath and aching. He held her close until he realized that he would never breathe normally again unless he let her go.

"I wouldn't want to be bad for business," Glory said, stepping backward, her hands automatically going to her hair to repin the strands that hadn't weathered the kiss.

Jared stopped her, shaking his head in reproach. "Leave it down, *healoha*. It suits you that way." His hands glided down her cheeks and over her neck to the collar of the brightly flowered blouse she wore under her plain dark suit. "This suits you, too," he said, his thumbs tracing her neck as his fingers fluffed the collar. He slid his hands under the jacket and slipped it over her arms. "This doesn't."

"You don't want me to look professional?"

He laughed like a man in pain. "Shall I tell you how I want you to look? What I want you to wear?"

She tried to smile. "I don't think you—"

"I want you to wear raindrops, sunlight and moonbeams. I want you to wear ecstasy on your face and my body on yours."

"Jared..." There was no ecstasy on her face at his words, only torment. "I can't—"

He silenced her with a finger against her lips. "I'm not asking you for anything now. But we both know it's only a matter of time."

She shut her eyes, suffused with heat and doubt—and anger at the people in the tiny secret village.

When she opened her eyes, Jared was gone.

The trip to the hidden valley took Glory longer than she had planned. The afternoon sun was high in the clouds overhead when she finally neared the place where the narrow canyon cut through the rocks.

She hadn't told anyone where she was going, but to be cautious, she had left a note on her desk, explaining her whereabouts. If she didn't come back that evening, she knew someone would find it and begin the search for her.

The note had only been a precaution, however. She didn't expect to have trouble. She planned to observe the homesteaders carefully before she ventured into their settlement. She was no fool; she knew that fierce sentiment existed against those who held vast tracts of Kauai. The island was a relatively peaceful place, but there were those capable of violence here just as there were anywhere else in the world.

She slowed Ghost to an amble, listening carefully as they moved along the path that led to the canyon. The path was overgrown and practically useless. If she and Peggy hadn't been experienced horsewomen, they would never have chosen it, but they had been tempted by views of the ocean along the way. From the path's condition, however, she guessed that no one else from Wehilani had come through in months.

She wondered how the homesteaders had known about the valley. It was possible that they had happened upon it as they searched for suitable land. But more likely the location had been passed down from father to son for generations. Perhaps it was or had once been a favorite location for hunting. Perhaps it had once been a sacred place and was even now filled with the ghosts and voices of the dead.

She slid from the saddle and led Ghost for the last hundred yards. She had heard no shouts, no sounds of any kind, but she didn't want to take any chances that she might find the homesteaders passing through the canyon. She stayed outside the entrance for several minutes, listening carefully, before she freed Ghost and began her journey through the rock passage.

The way was narrower and longer than she had remembered. She began to wonder what might happen if she found the homesteaders coming out as she ventured in. What would she say? And if they were angry at her discovery, what would she do?

She continued on, listening intently, until she came to the small clearing, which was the last resting place before entering the valley. She squatted, peering through the slim gap that was the only thing that stood between her and the village.

Everything was still. With her limited view, she had to move from side to side to determine whether the village was still inhabited. For a moment her heart soared at the possibility that the homesteaders had gone. If they had, she could tell Jared what she had found and not betray anyone. But just as she began to hope she had found a solution, she heard a faint bleating from the goat pen, and a brown billy, who had been lying in the dirt, stood and shook himself.

She felt a stab of disappointment that she still must make a choice. Jared or the homesteaders. Love or honor—except that it wasn't that clear-cut or noble. Her choice was impossible, because no matter what she chose, she lost something she needed to survive.

She stared desolately at the small settlement for long minutes. Just as she was beginning to believe that the goat was the only living thing in residence, a young woman emerged from one of the huts, a fat brown baby balanced on her hip.

She was very young and too thin, as if she had nourished the child to her own detriment. As she walked, the baby played with her long black braid. When she set the baby down in the middle of the clearing, it immediately rolled to its back on the rock-strewn ground and began to suck its toes.

As Glory watched, the child she had seen the first day, a small boy, came out of the hut and joined the baby in the clearing. Both children entertained themselves in the dirt as their mother went to what looked to be a storage shed near the goat's pen. She returned with a hoe and, gathering the baby once more on her hip, started toward the vegetable garden.

The toddler busied himself throwing rocks at nothing, and when he had tired of that, he started after his mother, who had placed the baby in a grassy circular pen built of large stones beside the garden.

Glory watched the young woman work. She was skilled with the hoe, chopping with a steady rhythm that spoke of hours of practice. Her strength—or lack of it—was a different matter. She rested often, wiping sweat from her forehead with the back of her hand, although the mountain air was cool enough that Glory wasn't really warm even though she was wearing a long-sleeved blouse.

The young woman reached the end of the row and stopped, sinking to the ground as if she could no longer stand. The toddler joined her there, crawling into her lap, and she laid her cheek on top of his hair. Glory guessed that she had closed her eyes in exhaustion.

Her mind made up, Glory squeezed through the narrow gap into the secret valley and started across the clearing.

She had almost reached the circular pen where the baby played with a rubber toy when the woman opened her eyes and saw Glory approaching.

"O wai 'oe?" The woman scrambled to her feet, and then, as if she realized she had spoken in Hawaiian, she repeated the question in English. "Who are you?"

Glory felt a stab of sadness for the fear and false bravado that had fueled the question. "A friend," she assured her. "Someone who won't hurt you, I promise."

The toddler, seeming to sense his mother's distress, disappeared behind her legs.

"Who are you?" the woman repeated.

Glory saw her sway. She hurried toward her, reaching her just as the woman's legs collapsed beneath her and she sank to the ground once more. Glory knelt beside her, touching her cheek.

"You're sick." The young woman's cheeks were blazing with fever. "Let me help you back inside."

"Who are you?" The question was weaker, but Glory knew she would continue to ask it until it was answered to her satisfaction.

"I'm Glory Kalia." She considered stopping there, but she knew the young woman would hound her until she told the whole truth. "I work at Wehilani. I'm the estate manager. I've known about this village for two weeks, and I haven't told anyone yet. You can trust me long enough to get you inside, can't you?"

"Hele aku!"

"I'm not going away, and you're going inside." Glory put her arm around the young woman's shoulders. "And you'd better know that I've got five brothers and sisters. I'm very good at getting what I want, no matter what it takes. Right now I want you in bed!"

The young woman drew a breath that was close to a sob. "Please, I..."

"Wikiwiki!" Glory slid her arm around the young woman's waist to hurry her and began to tug her to a standing position. "I'll take care of the *keikis* after I get you into bed." She hesitated. "Unless there's someone else here who you can call for help?"

"No."

Satisfied that they were alone except for the children, Glory succeeded in helping the young woman to her feet. "What's your name?" she asked as they started slowly toward the hut.

"Sara."

Glory didn't comment on the absence of a last name. She was surprised she had even gotten a first. "Sara, how long have you been sick?"

"I'm not sick. I just need to rest a little."

"You're burning up with fever."

"I'll be fine. Kapua went to gather some herbs to make me stronger."

"And did this Kapua person ask you to hoe the garden while she was gone?"

Sara stumbled and almost took Glory to the ground with her. "No."

They managed to stay upright, but Glory tightened her arm for support. "Then perhaps you were hoping to make your children into orphans?"

"No!"

They had almost reached the hut from which Sara had emerged. "I'm going to help you inside. Then you're going to lie down while I get the children. What are their names?" Glory looked behind her and saw that the toddler had crawled into the pen with the baby as if to protect it.

"The baby is Luana. My son is Kona."

"They're beautiful children, Sara. They deserve to have a mother, not a tombstone, to honor."

Sara seemed to sag at Glory's words. She let Glory help her into the hut and onto a crude bed that was built of rough boards, with folded blankets for a mattress. As primitive as it was, however, Sara seemed relieved to be in it.

Glory took a quick glance around the hut. The floor was constructed of flat rocks, laid side by side and covered with ti leaves woven into mats that served to keep dust at a minimum. The walls were unseasoned planks interlaced with ti and other fibers that seemed to do an adequate job of keeping out the wind. The room was almost bare except for a few small treasures: a white china bowl, a handmade quilt of red-and-white appliqué, a small dark wood cabinet with the unmistakable patina of age and tender care.

"I'll bring the children in," Glory promised as Sara pleaded wordlessly with her. "Then we'll talk."

Glory was almost to the stone circle when she realized she and the children were not alone. An older woman with short gray hair and a marked stoop had emerged from the woods bordering the garden. She carried a bundle of plants under one arm, and a gnarled staff under the other.

"Where's Sara?" she demanded, striding toward the children and reaching them before Glory could. She swung the baby to her hip, dropping her staff, before she turned to repeat her question. "Where is Sara?"

"She's inside. I told her I'd bring the children in."

"I've got them. Go away."

"I'm afraid I can't do that."

The old woman didn't answer. Instead she started toward the hut, leading the toddler by the hand. Glory followed behind. When they reached Sara's hut, Glory entered, too. Her Hawaiian was good enough to catch most of the rapid-fire conversation between Sara and the older woman, who was obviously Kapua, the herb gatherer Sara had mentioned earlier. Glory waited for a pause, then answered the questions Sara hadn't been able to, showing tactfully that she had understood them.

"As Sara's told you, I'm Glory Kalia, from Wehilani. This valley belongs to Jared Farrell, and since I manage this estate, I know you haven't asked for permission to farm the land." She paused, taking in Sara's tear-filled eyes and fever-flushed cheeks. "But all that can wait," she said. "Let's make Sara comfortable before we do any more talking. Kapua, were you going to make tea?"

Kapua gave a curt nod, turning back to Sara. "Did you take your pills like I told you to?"

"I did."

"And did you rest?"

Sara wouldn't answer.

Kapua sighed. "You won't get better if you insist on working."

"There's so much to do!"

"It will get done." Still carrying the baby, Kapua marched outside.

Glory followed. "Kapua, what's wrong with her? Has she seen a doctor?"

"Look around and you'll see what's wrong with her."

Glory pondered Kapua's answer. "You'll have to tell me," she said finally.

Kapua grunted. She bent to gather a pile of sticks together in the center of what was obviously their cooking area. The baby's weight threw her off balance, and she stumbled. Glory was at her side, lifting the baby from her arms before she could protest.

The baby, Luana, snuggled against her as if she were an old friend. Glory cooed softly, rocking her back and forth. Kapua watched for a moment, then, shrugging, bent once more to pile the sticks for a fire.

"Sara's never been well since Luana's birth. I told my son she wouldn't be able to live here this way. But my son, he's a stubborn man. He won't listen."

"Sara's running a fever."

"She catches everything. Ray thought that up here, with the mountain air and no people crowding her, she'd get better."

"Is that why you came?" Glory asked incredulously.

Kapua straightened long enough to give Glory a withering stare. "Does that seem like enough reason for you?"

"No." Glory knew she'd been chastened. Kapua wasn't a large woman, but she had the peculiar power of years mixed with knowledge that seemed to transcend size. Her leathery face was a road map of experiences. Glory yearned for a pencil to capture her on paper.

"We didn't come for Sara's health." Kapua reached into the pocket of her muumuu and took out a book of matches.

"Why did you come?"

"Because there was no place else to go." The fire was blazing brightly before Kapua stood. She started toward the storage shed while Glory waited. Kapua pulled out a black iron kettle and carried it to the stream that ran beside the taro patch. She filled it with water, and then, holding it against her midriff, started back across the clearing to suspend it on chains hanging from a metal pole across the camp fire. After rummaging in the voluminous pocket of her muumuu, she pulled out the bundle of herbs and threw half of them into the kettle.

Glory had stood patiently watching Kapua make tea. Silently she promised herself that she would never take an electric stove and a teakettle for granted again. "I grew up in a family with six children," she said softly when it was apparent that Kapua was going to say no more. "I thought I understood what it meant to have very little. But I don't understand what it means to have so little that you borrow another's land, knowing, all the time, that you might be caught."

"You tiptoe around the truth. We've stolen this land. Just as our land was stolen from us."

"Are you here to prove a point?"

"We're here because there was no place else to go."

Glory was afraid that Kapua was going to stop there once more. But after a moment the old woman continued.

"I have three sons. Our family has always farmed a plot near Hanapepe. We took care of ourselves. My oldest son fished, the other two farmed. We gave back to the land what it gave to us. Two months ago they brought in bulldozers and tore down our houses, our trees, our gardens. They're building tourist cottages there now."

Glory felt a chill, and she hugged the baby harder. "Kapua—"

Kapua held up her hand. "We stayed until the bulldozers came. Our neighbors stayed with us, but we couldn't stop the machines. So now we have no land, and we steal yours." She gestured around her. "My husband is dead, but he used to talk of this place. He had come here once to hunt, with his father. Ray is my youngest son. He found it for us."

Glory thought about Jared. Surely he would be touched by Kapua's story. But would he be touched enough to let her live here with her family? How long before the sons needed more land to feed their children? How long before others found their way to Wehilani? His privacy would be gone forever.

"You must have known someone would discover you," Glory said at last.

"We live one day at a time. Today we have a home. Tomorrow?" She shrugged. "Tomorrow this Mr. Farrell won't even need a bulldozer to get rid of us. He can tear down our houses with his hands, just like we put them up. Sara and my other *kaikamahines* can watch the little they salvaged last time be destroyed. I saved nothing. I will only lose my heart again."

"Mr. Farrell is a good man. If you went to him, maybe—"

"I know about the Farrells. Our land, the land we farmed for generations, was Farrell land. Then your Mr. Farrell's father sold it to another rich *haole*. We could barely pay our rent when the Farrells owned it. Later we had to save and go without to pay, until finally it was sold out from under us. We couldn't save to buy more land, even if there was more land to buy. What would this Jared Farrell do if I went to him? Do I have money? Does he understand any other kind of talk?"

Glory wanted to protest, yet she wondered if Kapua was right. When Jared had been unhappy about the world encroaching on land he owned, he had simply bought more. He solved his problems with his signature on a check. Would he understand what these people had suffered?

"If I've discovered you, others will find you, too," Glory said after the silence had gone on for too long.

Kapua stepped closer to the fire, stirring the contents of the kettle with a stick stripped of its bark. When she finished, she faced Glory. "You're not going to tell, are you?"

It was a statement. Glory saw surprise and dawning respect in Kapua's eyes. "I can't promise anything. You shouldn't be here. Sara should be closer to a doctor. All of you should be closer to town. What if something happened to one of the children?" She paused. "Are there other children besides these two?" At Kapua's slight nod she went on. "What about school, Kapua?"

"Do you think we plan to live here forever? Ray stays here, and my other daughters-in-law and their children. But my two oldest sons work down below. They sleep on the fishing boat. They save every penny and only visit us monthly. We will find a way out of here."

"Where are the others now?"

"Lola and Connie have taken their children down to visit their families. Ray went with them to get more medicine for Sara."

Glory thought about the grueling trip on foot down the mountain. It spoke of their desperation.

Kapua seemed to really look at Glory for the first time. "You're from Kauai?"

"My mother's family is."

"How can anyone own what once belonged to everyone? My ancestors lived in this valley once and in others just like it. Perhaps yours did, too. Can you hear their laughter? Their tears?"

Kapua's words were so like Glory's own comments to Jared the first day they had met that she had no response.

"We will stay now," Kapua said, turning back to her tea. "Until we find a way to leave or until your Mr. Farrell tears down our huts. What you do must be up to you."

Glory knew their conversation had ended. She turned back to the hut to tell Sara she was going. Inside, she found the young mother asleep, her arms locked defensively around her napping son. Glory backed out, almost colliding with Kapua.

"Aloha," Kapua said in farewell. *"A hui hou kakou."*

Until we meet again. "I won't come again," Glory said sadly. "But promise me that if Sara doesn't get better, you'll find a way to take her down the mountain or you'll come to Wehilani for help."

"Would it *help* for us to be homeless? That's what will happen if we go there."

"You've got to promise, or I'll tell Mr. Farrell the minute I get back."

Kapua lifted her head proudly. "I wouldn't risk Sara's life."

"Then you'll come to me for help if she's not better?"

"I'll come to you if I must. I will come to your Mr. Farrell when the mountains fall into the ocean."

"Jared Farrell is a good man."

Kapua laughed derisively. "Then tell me this, Glory Kalia. If he is such a good man, why are you afraid to tell him what you've found?"

When Glory had no answer, Kapua shook her head and disappeared inside the hut.

Glory took longer to ride back to Wehilani than she had planned. For the first miles she let Ghost have her head, ignoring both the sun sinking toward the highest mountaintops and the deepening chill in the air. She was so immersed in her thoughts that a pale moon shone in the sky by the time she realized she had to spur Ghost on or risk losing her way.

She reached the main path by the fading rays of twilight. Ghost picked up her pace naturally, sensing that One Leg would be waiting in the stables with oats and a rubdown. Glory encouraged the mare to move even faster, hoping that she could get to her room without encountering Jared.

Only the tack room light was burning when they arrived. Glory imagined that One Leg was up at the house having his supper. She slid from the saddle and opened the door, leading Ghost inside. Demon whinnied a greeting, and the other horses moved restlessly in their stalls, as if they yearned to be outside on this fine cool night.

Glory dropped the mare's reins and stroked her nose. "Stand still, girl, and I'll take off your saddle. Then I'll see what One Leg wants me to do with you," she crooned.

"I'll take care of her."

Glory spun around to see the tall dark figure of a man emerging from Demon's stall. He had started toward her before she realized it was Jared. "I didn't know anyone was here!"

"Well, if I scared you, *healoha*, it's no more than you deserve. Where have you been? I was just getting ready to search for you."

Glory felt such a flood of longing to be in Jared's arms that for a moment she almost told him the truth. She watched him move toward her, his stride purposeful, his expression a curious mixture of relief and irritation. All she had to do was tell him that she had ridden to the valley and seen the homesteaders. Then there would be no secrets between them.

And the homesteaders would have no home. Again.

"I..." Both the truth and a lie stuck in her throat. Instead, her answer was somewhere in between. "I've been exploring. The sun was almost behind the mountains when I realized how late it had gotten."

"Exploring?" He moved closer. "That's why you couldn't come to the beach house with me today?"

Slowly, inexorably, he was forcing her toward an answer she couldn't give. She searched for a response that would reassure him without a lie. She searched in vain.

Jared watched her struggle. "You just didn't want to come with me, did you?"

"Jared, I..." Her voice trailed off. To her chagrin, her eyes stung with tears.

"I know, Glory." He stepped forward and pulled her into his arms.

Glory rested against his chest even though she knew she shouldn't. Whatever he thought he knew, she was sure it wasn't the truth. But his arms felt so wonderful around her that she couldn't pull away.

"I had some time to think," he said, his lips against her hair. "I know what you must be feeling."

He couldn't possibly know, and she made a small sound of distress.

She felt him begin to stroke her hair. "You need more than I've offered, don't you *healoha*?"

She was confused but unable to break the spell of his voice and his hands. Behind her, Ghost whinnied at this break in her familiar routine.

"You need love," Jared said quietly.

Glory pulled away, searching his eyes. "I haven't asked you for anything."

"You make no demands, but you come into my arms so sweetly, I know what you feel."

She wasn't sure where he was leading, but she saw her chance to break free of him. Later, when he discovered her deceit, there would be no bonds to sever. She would break free now, before she could destroy them both.

"You're mistaken," she said, her words barely audible. She realized she had just uttered her first lie. She felt faint with the effort it had taken.

"No, I'm not."

"You're a very fine man, Jared, a very attractive man. It's lonely here, and we've both tried to push that loneliness away. But we're not right for each other. We have to stop this now before I lose my job because of it."

Jared frowned as if he were trying to read the emotions behind her words. "I don't believe you," he said finally.

"You've got no choice."

"No?" His mouth twisted into the semblance of a smile. "Shall I test my theory?"

Her eyes widened, and she backed up until Ghost was nuzzling her neck. "Please don't."

He advanced slowly. "You forget. I'm a man who never quits until he has the answer he's seeking."

"I've given you your answer."

"And now I require proof." His arm shot out, gripping her shoulder. "Show me you're just pushing loneliness away."

Glory felt herself being propelled toward the wall. "Jared! No!" She wasn't frightened of him; she was frightened of her own response. Already her knees trembled at the thought of what was to come.

"Or are you just a tease like my beloved *ex*-fiancée? Do you want me down on my hands and knees crawling for you?"

Glory flattened her palms against his chest, but she might as well have tried to hold back a tidal wave. She felt the wall behind her back just as his mouth claimed hers.

He was all hard muscle and harder determination. This was no careful wooing, no gentle exploration. His hands molded her bottom, forcing her against him as his tongue plunged repeatedly into her mouth. She was awash in sorrow that it had come to this, but the sorrow changed swiftly into passion.

She couldn't get enough of him. Somewhere, under the spontaneous combustion of desire, was the desperation of a woman hopelessly in love with a man who would soon have only contempt for her. For that moment, as wrong as it was, she gave in to her feelings. There were no lies now, only her body bursting into flames, her mouth hungrily joined with his.

He made a sound that could have been a growl or an oath. He pushed her harder against the wall as he began to fumble with the buttons on her blouse. She made no move to stop him. When it was half-undone and he had unfastened her bra, she still made no move.

She moaned when his hand covered her breast. He lifted the soft flesh and molded it as he kissed her. His thumb traced ever-narrowing circles around her nipple, until finally he brushed it once, then again. He grunted triumphantly as she melted so close that there were no boundaries between them, only one yearning, aching wish for fulfillment.

"Lonely, *healoha*? This isn't loneliness." He laughed derisively as she tried to protest. "Your body tells me what you won't. Your lips tell me." He claimed her other breast and listened to her faint cry. "Every inch of you tells me. I could take you here on the stable floor and you wouldn't stop me."

"No..."

"A challenge?" He laughed again, but the sound was tormented. "You would lose." He pressed against her, and she felt the heated stab of his flesh against her abdomen. He lifted her until she cradled him between her legs. "Tell me you know it."

"We would both lose," she said. She was trembling so hard she could only cling to him for support. "Please, Jared, this isn't right."

"Doesn't it feel right?" He pressed harder against her, and his lips tugged at her earlobe. "Tell me you don't want me to touch you. Let me hear you lie again."

She never cried, but she was crying now. "Please, Jared..."

"What are you asking me for?"

She couldn't answer, because there was no answer. She wanted to ask him for forgiveness, to beg him to help Sara, Kapua and the others. She wanted to plead with him to let her into his heart as he had found his way into hers. But she couldn't.

"Let me go," she said brokenly. "You're mistaken about what you think I feel."

He stepped back, lifting her face to examine the tears streaming down her cheeks. "Do you cry easily?" he asked cynically. "Patsy could turn her tears on and off as quickly as a summer thundershower."

She cringed at the comparison, but she couldn't deny that she was like the woman he had almost married. Patsy had pretended she was something she was not. Glory knew she was guilty of the same. With unsteady hands she wiped the tears from her face. "Are you finished with me yet?"

He dropped his hands to his side and stepped back. "Yes, *Miss Kalia*," he said, stressing her name. "I'm finished."

She waited for him to tell her that she was fired, but instead he turned his back to her. "I'll unsaddle Ghost. Go up to the house. Tell One Leg to get down here when he's finished his dinner."

She was almost out the door when his next words stopped her. "You still have a job at Wehilani. I won't have you claiming sexual harassment and dragging me through the courts. Just stay out of my way. Do you understand?''

She understood that if she left now, there would be no one to plead the cause of the homesteaders when they were discovered. For a moment she balanced her own need to flee with their need for defense. They had already cost her so much.

''Unless you don't want to work here,'' he added when she didn't answer.

She didn't want to stay at Wehilani, but she also realized she wasn't ready to say goodbye to Jared, either. Perhaps after weeks of his disdain she would be able to let go of even this tenuous tie. Perhaps then she would no longer have the homesteaders on her conscience. Until that moment, staying at Wehilani would be excruciating but necessary.

''I'll stay.'' She was surprised she could sound so normal.

''I'm having houseguests next week for Friday and Saturday night. I've invited ten. See that all the guest rooms are ready and meals are planned. I want a party of some kind on Saturday night. The rest is up to you. I don't want to be consulted about details.''

''I'll take care of it.''

''I'm sure you will, Miss Kalia. You're very good at anything that doesn't require any feeling.''

She stumbled out into the cool night air, but even the light wind tossing the branches of the silver oak grove behind the stables couldn't dry the new tears that slid down her cheeks.

Chapter Nine

Jared's pencil snapped in half. The sound echoed through the tomblike silence of his laboratory like a cannon blast. He hurled the pieces across the room into the only wastebasket that wasn't overflowing with trash and listened for the satisfying ping of wood against metal before he wrenched open his desk drawer for a replacement.

There was no replacement. The drawer, like everything in the lab, was a disaster area. He slammed it shut and stood, running his fingers through his hair until it was a disaster area, too.

The broken pencil didn't really matter, and he knew it. He was tempted to rant and rave, kick furniture, throw anything he could get his hands on, but when he was finished, he knew that the painful feelings bottled up inside him would still be there, just as they'd been there since the night he'd confronted Glory in the stables.

Glory. She was impossible to forget, because everything reminded him of her. And if that wasn't bad enough, she seemed to be everywhere he looked. Now, as he stood staring out the window in front of his desk, he saw her with two workmen, parading in and out of the old gazebo, gesturing toward the newly repaired roof as if she were sweetly admonishing them for some detail they had overlooked.

He didn't know what detail it could be. She was a meticulous taskmaster. Paradox had confided that the workmen called her *mano u'i*, "beautiful shark," when she wasn't around to hear them. Everyone respected her, though, because she never showed irritation in any way. She encouraged them with her soft musical voice and innocently seductive smile. Then she demonstrated how hard they should work by working that hard herself.

Jared had gotten a bargain when Glory Kalia was hired as estate manager. Only it was a bargain that was costing him pieces of his heart and fragments of his soul.

She was also costing him his concentration. The design he was working on was as skillfully wrought as a three-year-old's crayon portrait. His gaze flicked to the blueprints spread like the daily news over his desk. In the past week and a half he had accomplished nothing. He fought the urge rising inside him, but lost. With one vicious sweep of his hand blueprints decorated the floor and the desktop was bare of anything except dust.

Jared turned on his heel and stalked out of the room.

Outside, Wehilani mist colored the air like thousands of tiny rainbows glistening in the sunlight. The estate had never looked lovelier. Glory had persuaded the workmen to perform miracles with paint and saws, clippers and rakes. He wondered if she had also bargained with the heavens to make this day, the day his guests were to arrive, one of the most beautiful of the year.

Jared gave a cynical grunt. He couldn't care less what kind of day it was. He didn't feel like a party.

He skirted the gazebo and was heading toward the house when he heard Glory call him. He was tempted to ignore her, but he had already behaved like a child in his laboratory. Now he steeled himself not to show any of the feelings streaming through him at the sound of her voice. He had behaved like a hurt child, but he wasn't a child. He was a man.

A man in love with a woman who didn't want him.

He turned and forced himself to speak calmly. "What is it, Glory?"

She stopped just in front of him, opening her mouth to speak. She closed it, then moistened her lips as if to help ease the words out. "You haven't called me by my first name in a long time."

That delicate sweep of her tongue, combined with the words he knew she hadn't intended to say, was almost his undoing. He commanded himself not to react. "I'm on my way up to the house. What do you need?"

"I...I know you asked me not to consult you about anything, but..."

He wondered how eyes so dark could show such hurt. For a moment he almost believed it was real. Then he remembered how thoroughly she had rejected him. She had made it clear that she had no feelings toward him. The pain was obviously manufactured. "Apologies waste time," he said curtly. "What is it?"

Her eyelids fluttered shut. When she opened them, no emotion showed on her face. "I wouldn't want to waste your time," she said softly. "I just want to be sure you approve of the party I've planned."

He waved her words aside. "I don't care what you do."

"It's a luau." She rushed on before he could stop her. "The evenings have been so beautiful that I thought you'd want to have something outdoors. Entertainment's scheduled, and Lucy is preparing a feast."

"I told you I don't care."

"Jared..." She reached out and touched his arm. He felt as cold and stiff as a marble statue. "Please. I can't go on like this."

Her fingers felt as if they were burning right through to his bones. "Like what?"

"Can't we be friends again?"

"Is that what we were?" He shook off her hand, but his chilling gaze pinned her to the spot where she stood. "Friends?"

"Surely never more than that. You never claimed more and—"

"I never had the chance to claim more." He laughed a little, but the sound died as hurt crept back into her eyes. "You were very good at heading me off, Glory. Your timing was commendable."

She looked as if he had slapped her.

Jared couldn't face another minute of this. He wanted to pull her into his arms and kiss the hurt from her face, and he knew how disastrous that would be. "Is there anything else?" he asked gruffly.

"Are you saying that . . ." Her voice trailed off, but her eyes pleaded with him.

"Am I saying that I was falling in love with you?" She didn't nod, but Jared saw the answer in her eyes. He saw no reason to tell her the truth. Sometime during the afternoon he'd spent at the beach house without her, he had realized that he loved her. That night, in the stables, he had been working up the courage to tell her. Now he saw no reason to. What would the truth bring except humiliation for both of them?

He forced a laugh. "You said it yourself. We were both lonely. I guess I should be glad you saw it so clearly. At least you didn't try to make me believe you were in love with me. You're honest, and you kept me from being a complete fool."

"Honest?"

He could barely hear her. "What?"

"Honest?" She shook her head. Then, without another word, she turned and ran down the path toward the house.

Jared watched her go, pain contorting his face. Why, after everything that had passed between them, did he still want to go after her?

The answer was simple. Despite everything he had just said, he was still in love with her. He was a man who never seemed to learn.

In the middle of the afternoon, Sally tracked Glory down. "I've been looking for you for hours! Jared says to tell you that we've got two more guests coming."

Glory turned at Sally's words and struggled to smile. For once the housekeeper wasn't dramatizing the truth. Glory had stayed out of everyone's way after her confrontation with Jared. Even now she could hardly go through the motions of a normal conversation.

She forced herself to try. "Well, there'll be plenty to eat, but I'm afraid I'm going to have to put them up in the O.K. Corral." She hesitated. "We are talking about a husband and wife, I hope."

Sally looked down at her list. "Looks like it. A Mr. and Mrs. Cole Chandler. The O.K. Corral?"

"Cole and Toby?" Glory let the news sink in. She hadn't expected her friends to be two of Jared's guests. For a moment the need for someone to confide in almost overwhelmed her. Toby, crazy, loony Toby, would understand what she had done.

"The O.K. Corral?" Sally repeated.

"The bedroom in the rear of the west wing. The one where I hung all those Western paintings that used to be in my office."

Sally nodded. "I already got it ready, just in case this happened. Jared said he'd invited the Chandlers right at the start, but they didn't think they could come. Their son was sick."

"Nicky was sick?" For a moment Glory forgot her own misery. In typical Sally-style, the words "their son was sick" had conveyed a life-threatening illness.

"Cutting a tooth, I think he said, but he's better now. They're bringing him with them, so we're supposed to set up a crib in their room."

Relieved, Glory forced another smile. "There's one in the attic, isn't there?"

"I'll get Paradox to bring it down." Sally started down the hall.

"And the high chair," Glory called after her.

"There's a box of toys, too. I'll be sure they're clean."

The formal halls of Wehilani were going to be brightened by a child's laughter. For a moment Glory shut her eyes and tried to imagine the sound. There was nothing as pure, as soul lifting. Nicky was a special child. Graced with his mother's ebullience and his father's sensitivity, he charmed everyone he met. He would bring life to Wehilani.

Just as Jared's own children would someday.

Glory wasn't surprised at the sharp pain that thought caused her. Pain had carved a deep well where once there had been love and warmth. She prayed that soon there would be nothing left inside her that could feel pain or sorrow or regret.

Regret was the worst of all. She longed to start again, and yet she didn't know what she would change. Could she live with herself if she was responsible for the eviction of the homesteaders? Would she close her eyes at night and see their faces instead of Jared's? Would she read condemnation in the eyes of every Hawaiian she met, even if there was none?

Now the condemnation she saw was in Jared's eyes. She knew what he thought of her. She had led him on, made him unspoken promises—then she had denied them. At best he believed she was confused and immature, at worst that she was like Patsy, a woman who promised everything and delivered nothing.

And what would he think of her when he discovered the homesteaders? Would he see her struggle? Understand the courage it had taken to hide the truth? Or would he see only that she had lied?

She knew the answer. She had chosen the homesteaders over him. That would be the only truth apparent to Jared.

"Miss Glory?"

Glory opened her eyes to see Paradox standing there, a frown of concern on his face.

"Are you all right?" he asked.

For a moment she was tempted to say no, to throw herself into the Oriental giant's arms and accept his sympathy. Instead she mustered a nod. "I'm fine. Maybe just a little tired."

"I'll talk to you later, then. When you're rested."

Glory knew there would be no later. Once the guests began to arrive, she would be busy every moment. And afterward she was leaving Wehilani. Today she had learned that she could no longer bear the pain. She wouldn't be here to plead the cause of the homesteaders when they were discovered, but perhaps that would be best for them, anyway. She had no influence with Jared any longer. She might even prejudice him against them.

"Tell me now," she encouraged Paradox. "I'm fine. Really."

He looked as if he didn't believe her, but he nodded. "Lucy and I are getting married. The weekend after next."

As badly as she felt, her smile was genuine. She gave him a quick hug. "I'm so happy for you."

"Mr. Jared's given us permission to have the ceremony here."

"It will be beautiful."

"We'd like you to be there, of course."

"Thank you." Glory didn't want to tell Paradox that she was leaving, before she told Jared. She responded without making a commitment. "You know I wish you both the very best."

Paradox cleared his throat. "There is one problem. Sally and Rolfe are taking their vacation then. Lucy and I were going to stay here after the wedding, but Mr. Jared insists we go on a honeymoon."

Glory watched a blush steal over the big man's features. "I think he's right," she agreed.

"That will only leave One Leg and you to take care of the place."

She didn't correct him. "I'm sure Wehilani's withstood worse."

"I believe I hear the first helicopter arriving."

Glory listened closely and heard the telltale whir, too. "I guess we'd better go greet the guests."

"Miss Glory?"

She turned back. "Yes?"

"If you're having a problem—" Paradox cleared his throat again "—anyone here would be glad to help. We've always been a family, and you're part of it now."

Tears stung her eyes. "Thanks," she said huskily. "But I'm afraid no one can help with this." She realized as she said the words that they were true. Even Toby wouldn't be able to help her. She was on her own, and the best she could hope for was that she could leave Wehilani before she broke under the strain.

Toby, Cole and Nicky arrived in the fourth helicopter load. They were almost the last guests. Only one man, John Clemens, a physician from Honolulu, remained to be picked up at the airport in Lihue that evening.

First out, Toby crossed the yard toward Glory, talking as she did. "You've lost weight and you're too pale. What is Jared doing to you, anyway?" Toby kissed Glory's cheek and thrust Nicky into her arms, sure that he would be welcome there. She frowned suddenly. "What *could* a man do to a woman to make her lose weight? Jared might make another million if he patents it."

Glory was used to Toby's flights of thought. She hugged Nicky to her, overwhelmed by his sweet baby scent and cuddly flesh. He pulled her long braid over her shoulder and began to babble. "I'm so glad you're here," she told Toby, not quite meeting her eyes. "I've missed you."

Toby was still frowning. "I can see that. Nola's going to come up here, you know, and personally make sure you gain back the weight you've lost."

"Mama won't come because she won't ride a horse and she's deathly afraid of heights, so the chopper's out. And stop talking about my weight. I'm fine."

"Isn't Toby behaving?" Cole joined them, bending to kiss Glory's cheek. He straightened, but behind his I-promise-not-to-intrude facade, Glory could see concern. She wondered if what she had suffered really showed that plainly.

"Toby spends too much time with Mama." Glory buried her face in Nicky's shining curls for a moment, afraid she was going to give in to the tears that always seemed to be just below the surface now.

She looked up in time to see Toby and Cole exchanging worried looks. "Look, I'm fine. Aren't I allowed to be a little sentimental when my two...three—" she looked down at Nicky and attempted a smile "—best friends come to visit?"

Cole interrupted Toby, effectively blocking whatever response she had been about to give. "Sure you are. We're glad to see you, too. Now tell me, where's Jared?"

"He's with some of the other guests. How about letting me show you to your room, and then you can find him?"

Upstairs, she waited until she was sure that the Chandlers had everything they needed; then, swiftly handing a cheerful Nicky back to his mother, she made her escape, promising that she would see them later.

She didn't hear Cole's next words, spoken into a surprisingly silent room.

"When I find Jared Farrell, I'm going to wring his neck."

Nor Toby's response.

"The man won't even have a neck if *I* find him first."

Jared strode across the crowded living room to greet Toby and Cole, who had just come down the stairs. He was truly glad to see them. Most of the people he had invited were business acquaintances, but Toby and Cole were friends. And he needed friends.

He extended his hand to Cole and bent to kiss Toby. It was only after their perfunctory greetings that he noticed neither of them was smiling.

"Where's the baby?" he asked. "Is he all right?"

"Nicky's sleeping upstairs," Toby answered.

"Is anything the matter?"

Neither one answered him, but Jared got the distinct feeling that he had suddenly become Exhibit A and they were the jury.

He had never seen Toby without a welcoming smile. She was a petite dynamo with eyes the color of spring wheat and tousled curls the color of rich Kansas earth. Cole called her "Sunflower," and he had once lovingly described her to Jared as both dingbat and sage. She projected a fresh, wholesome innocence that allowed her to get away with saying anything that came to her mind—and almost anything might.

Cole, on the other hand, was dignified and aloof, the quintessential Boston Brahmin. He adored Toby, a gust of fresh air in a life that had known little, and when he was with her he showed his deep sensitivity and warmth. His tall broad-shouldered body, sun-streaked brown hair and deep tan might seem like the marks of a North Shore surfer, but Cole was a computer genius who had dedicated his life to building computers that would captivate and educate children. He and Toby lived in a villa near the Aikane Hotel, which she still managed, and as different as they were, they were also as well matched as two people could be.

"Apparently I've missed something," Jared said at last. "Are you going to let me in on what you're thinking? Innocent before being proved guilty and all that."

Toby opened her mouth to speak, and Cole clamped his hand firmly on her shoulder. "I think you and I need to have a talk," he told Jared. "As soon as possible."

Jared shrugged. "How about now? I'll show you the stables."

"Fine." Cole tightened his fingers to keep Toby quiet. "You'll stay here, won't you, Sunflower?"

She pried his fingers loose. "I'll be in the kitchen getting an ice pack for my shoulder."

The two men were outside before Cole spoke again. "Glory met our chopper when we arrived."

"Competent, isn't she?"

Cole exploded, surprising them both. "She looks like hell!"

"Impossible." Jared stopped and faced his friend. "But spit it out. What are you trying to say?"

"You want it simple? I want to know what you've done to her."

Jared ticked off the signs that told him Cole was furious: the pulse throbbing noticeably in Cole's neck, the hands that were curled into fists, the coiled stance of a man about to spring. He weighed them all against Cole's inbred dignity, then turned and started walking toward the stables. "Nothing," he said. "Not a damn thing. Her virtue's intact, if that's what's worrying you."

Cole grabbed his arm. For a moment Jared tensed, waiting for Cole to swing. Then Cole's hands dropped to his sides. "You sound like a real cold-blooded—"

"I'm not." Jared saw the deep concern in Cole's eyes, and strangely, despite Cole's anger, he knew some of that concern was for him. "I'm in love with her," he said before the words had time to be tested and blotted out. "And the feeling's not mutual."

Cole looked like a man who had been ready to take a mighty leap only to find that the place he was standing was best. "I don't believe it," he said finally.

Jared started walking again. "What don't you believe? That Glory could resist my charms? That I could fall in love with the most beautiful woman in the islands? Both happened. Glory's made it very clear that whatever she feels for me, it's not love. As to why you sensed all this after one meeting with her, I don't know. She has nothing to feel badly about. Her job's not in danger. I'm not going to throw myself at her."

Cole tried to put everything Jared was saying together. "I till don't buy it."

"Why not?"

"Haven't you looked at her, Farrell? She's lost weight. he's got circles under her eyes. She held on to Nicky today ke he was her last hope for salvation. This isn't a woman ho's trying to let a man down gently. This is a woman eing eaten alive by something."

"I've tried *not* to look at her, damn it! I look at her and see everything I've ever wanted. If I don't look at her I can retend . . ."

"Pretend what?"

Jared laughed scornfully. "I can pretend that she's not hat I thought she was. It's my way of coping."

"She's everything you ever thought she was and more."

"Maybe. Maybe not. I don't know anymore."

"Since when did lying to yourself help anything?" Cole sked gently.

"Since I met Glory Kalia." Jared opened the stable door nd ushered his friend inside.

Cole stopped in the doorway. "That answer's got a lot in ommon with the smell in here."

"I'm afraid it's the only answer I've got," Jared said arkly. "If Glory's got a different one, she's keeping it to erself."

Glory stood in the shadows of the lanai as the last heli-opter arrived. Jared stood not fifteen feet from her, but hey hadn't exchanged a word. He would greet Dr. Clem-ns, and she would show him to the room that had been repared for him. Then, if she was lucky, she would be done or the night.

She had spent the past week and a half trying not to look t Jared. Now she couldn't avoid it. She drank in the arro-ant set of his shoulders, the lean length of his legs, the leanly molded lines of his profile. She buried her finger-ips in her palms, remembering the feel of his hair sifting through her fingers, the cool, smooth texture of his skin. His mouth . . .

She had spent the afternoon performing her job like smiling robot, staying away from Jared and making hi guests as comfortable as possible. She had stayed away fron Toby and Cole, too, finding little tasks that needed her at tention each time they started toward her. She was coun ing the hours until the house party ended and she could fle Wehilani. Perhaps someday she would confide in Toby, bu now she could only keep her emotions under close guar and pray she made it until Sunday.

The noisy whir of the chopper preceded any other sign o it. Finally lights materialized out of the twilight. Normall Dave didn't fly this late in the day. Kauai's mountains wer tricky, even for a man who had flown medical rescue mis sions under enemy fire in Vietnam. Without being told t Glory had prepared a spare bedroom on the third floor fo him. Jared wouldn't want Dave to fly back in the dark.

"Why are there two people getting out of the back of th chopper?"

Surprised at Jared's words, Glory squinted into th deepening gloom brightened only by floodlights that illu minated the heliport.

His next word was even more surprising. "Damn!"

She wondered how one muttered oath could carry a life time of condemnation. As she strained to see, Jared starte forward. She followed at a safe distance.

They were still yards from the guests when she recog nized herself—only the woman walking toward her wasn' really her, of course. She wasn't a twin, either, but on firs impression she was so similar in appearance that Glor could only stare.

Jared ignored the woman, extending his hand to the ma walking beside her. "John," he said coldly. "I see you'v brought a friend."

Dr. John Clemens, a dignified man who looked as if h carried his medical bag everywhere he went, appeared be wildered. "Friend?"

"He means me," the woman cooed, gazing adoringly into John's face.

John laughed uncomfortably. "I don't get it."

Jared explained. "I'm referring to your traveling companion here. I didn't know you'd be bringing Patsy with you."

"You might say it was a spur-of-the-moment thing," Patsy said, focusing her considerable charm on Jared. "Please don't be angry at John."

Glory concentrated on the grim line of Jared's mouth as she took in the fact that Patsy Hightower was standing in front of her. Jared's recent history—alive and well.

"It must have been spur-of-the-moment," Jared said.

John seemed to be trying to break free of confusion. "I'm not sure what's going on here. . . ."

"You can't possibly begrudge me the chance to join your little party," Patsy said, pouting a little. "Besides, you'll need a hostess, Jared. Someone to help you put your guests at ease. You know how well I can do that."

"Like a cobra in a laboratory full of little white mice." Still staring coldly at Patsy, Jared inclined his head toward John. "Besides, I'm sure your date for the weekend wouldn't like you playing hostess for me."

"Hold on." John seemed to finally get a handle on what was happening. "Patsy's not my date. We just happened to ride up here in the same helicopter. We had dinner together last week, and we talked about the party. I told her I'd be the last one flown in tonight, and she volunteered to delay her arrival and fly up with me to keep me company."

"Delay her arrival?"

Dave joined them, a suitcase in each hand. "I didn't know I'd be bringing an extra guest, Jared. I didn't have room for all the supplies I was supposed to bring up. I'll have to go down first thing in the morning."

"You'll be taking Miss Hightower back with you," Jared said. "She won't be staying."

If poor John Clemens was rightfully confused about what was happening, Jared no longer was. The answer was clear to him. Patsy had learned about the party from John, pretended she had an invitation, too, and then acted as if she were John's date when they both arrived at the airport. Naturally Dave hadn't questioned her presence under the circumstances. It was typical manipulative Patsy.

Jared spotted Glory standing just at the edge of the heliport lights. He had the curious sensation of seeing her for the first time. He signaled her to come stand beside him.

Glory walked slowly toward him, but Patsy was paying no attention. "Jared," she said, touching his arm in a vain attempt to get him to turn back to her. "Let's not quibble about how I got here. I want to stay. And you could use my help, couldn't you? It's time we had a chance to talk. . . ."

Her voice trailed off as she saw Glory. For a moment Patsy looked as if she'd been struck by an eighteen-wheeler.

Jared casually laid his arms across Glory's shoulders. "Glory, do we have room for Patsy for the night?"

Glory knew she was being used to put Patsy in her place, but for that moment she wanted nothing more than to go along with the charade. Having Jared hold her close, even under these circumstances, was a reprieve from the loneliness to come.

"There's a room on the third floor ready for Dave," she said, sorting through the arrangements in her mind. "I'm afraid it's anything but plush, but if Dave doesn't mind bunking over the stables with One Leg tonight, Patsy can have it."

"Dave?" Jared asked.

Dave shrugged.

"Then, *healoha*, will you show her to her room please?"

The endearment was almost Glory's undoing. Her eyes flashed to Jared's. There was warmth there, laced with pain. For the first time she knew how much she had hurt him, and she longed to begin again. *I'm not like Patsy,* she wanted to shout. *Nothing like her. I can be trusted.* Only, of course, she couldn't be, and that was the thing she couldn't change.

She realized everyone was waiting for an answer. "Of course." Glory felt Jared squeeze her shoulder in thanks.

Patsy stepped forward. Her forehead was wrinkled in a rown. "We haven't been introduced."

"No. But I've heard of you," Glory answered. "I was ven mistaken for you once."

Patsy tossed her head. "I can see why."

Jared looked at the two women. There were similarities, ut they stopped at insignificant details like size and color-ng. The important things—integrity, sensitivity, warmth—hone in full measure in Glory's midnight eyes. Patsy's eyes, he same velvet black, were empty.

Seeing Patsy and Glory together was a revelation. Jared's eart suddenly felt a hundred pounds lighter. Whatever had nade Glory back away from him, it hadn't been a heartless ame. Something else was wrong, something that was caus-ng the circles under her eyes and the sadness in them. omething that could be changed. For the first time he be-ieved that whatever had gone wrong between him and the voman beside him could be set right.

And he wasn't going to rest until it was.

"Only a fool wouldn't see the differences between you," ared said before Glory could answer. He brushed his cheek gainst Glory's hair, and when she turned, he kissed her. 'And I am no longer a fool," he whispered, only for her ars. "So take warning."

Chapter Ten

She couldn't sleep.

Outside, rain fell like silver needles, transforming the thick midnight fog into the sheerest gossamer lace. The gentle patter against Glory's windowpanes should have soothed her, but tonight it seemed to pound to the rhythm of words she couldn't forget.

"Take warning."

She sat up and covered her face with her hands, her hair sliding over her shoulders to pool in her nightgown-covered lap. She had tossed restlessly for an hour. It was apparent that sleep wasn't going to come. She could lie in bed all night and continue trying to force something that couldn't be. Or she could get up and admit defeat.

"Take warning," she whispered. There had been a possessive gleam in Jared's eyes as he'd made the threat. And of what was she to be warned? If he truly believed that she and Patsy were nothing alike, what did that mean?

She had passed the point where anything made sense to her. The hour was late, but more than that, her emotions had been stretched, twisted and tied into knots for so long that she could no longer carry a thought to any sort of conclusion. There was no cloak of serenity to hide behind now. The cloak was gone, and the exposed woman was wounded and bleeding.

Glory swung her legs to the side of the bed and stood. She didn't know where she would go; she only knew that she had to go somewhere. Her nightgown fell to the floor in a snowy swirl as she pulled on a long-sleeved muumuu.

The house was quiet. The guests had all been tired from their long trips, retiring early. The staff knew they had a full day tomorrow and had retired early, too. Glory's footsteps seemed as loud as thunder in the empty hallways as she made her way to the rear stairway. She left the house through the kitchen without hearing another sound.

The rain was still falling. The narrow roof of the lanai protected her from the worst of the shower, but the thick mist dampened her skin immediately. She didn't want to stay close to the house, but the rain barred her from the long walk she ached for. Compromising, she slipped off her sandals and let the wet grass caress her feet as she ran toward the gazebo.

The soft symphony of raindrops was accompanied by the lonely call of a night bird. In the darkness, with rain bathing her skin and the heady smells and textures of a Wehilani night filling all her senses, she could almost forget what had made her flee her room. She could feel layers of time peel back, one by one, until she was transformed into a village maiden, running through the dark rain forest night of old Kauai to meet her lover.

He was a king, a mountain chief, and she was a beautiful lowborn island girl. They could never be one in marriage, just as the flowers of the naupaka would never grown whole and full, but for this night only they could be together.

She saw the picture clearly in her mind, just as in her drawings of Leilehua and Hakuole, she and Jared were the man and the woman.

She slowed to a stop beneath the shelter of the golden shower trees that ringed the octagonal gazebo, shaking what rain she could from her clothes before she opened one of the screened doors and went inside. She stood quietly, letting her eyes adjust to the dimmer light.

"Did my thoughts call you here?"

She drew back against the door, startled. "Jared?"

He stepped out of the shadows, closer to a window, and she could just make out his silhouette. "I watched you run across the lawn. Were you looking for me?"

She couldn't answer. She *had* been looking for him, although she hadn't known it and she hadn't expected to find him. She knew she would look for Jared forever, in the face of each man she met, in the warmth of a smile, the dark flash of eyes.

"Glory?" He moved toward her, melting from shadow into light until he stood just in front of her.

"I couldn't sleep. I didn't know you were here."

"Didn't you?" He brushed her hair back from her face with his fingers. "I knew you'd come."

"No." She barely breathed the word.

"You're wet." One hand stroked her cheek. Reflexively Glory turned her face toward it like an infant seeking its mother's warmth. "Couldn't you sleep?" he asked.

She shook her head.

"Neither could I."

"I should go." Her voice was low and shaky.

"No." Jared slipped his arms around her and pulled her against him. "I don't want you to until we've talked."

"There's nothing we—"

"I love you."

"You can't!" Glory tried to pull free, but Jared held her tightly. "You don't know me well enough to love me, Jared."

"I feel like I've known you forever. I think I loved you the first time I saw you."

"I reminded you of Patsy! You were still getting over your feelings for her, and I looked like her."

He held her just far enough away to see her eyes. In the ear darkness he could still see fear and sorrow in their epths.

"There was nothing to get over. Patsy was a lovely diver-on. I tried to convince myself that there could be more. She ied to convince me, too. At the end she wasn't even a di-ersion, just another woman who couldn't be trusted."

His words were a knife twisting inside her. Jared could el it as sharply as if it were his own body crying out in ain. "What is it?" he demanded. "And don't tell me you on't care for me. I almost believed you last time, but I can't e fooled twice."

"We're not right for each other." The words caught in her roat even though she believed them. "Sometimes what vo people feel isn't enough."

"Two people?"

"You're confusing me. I didn't mean—"

"Do you love me, Glory?" Jared slid his hands up her eck to frame her face, forcing her eyes to his. "Look at me hen you answer."

She couldn't, and yet she had no choice. She parted her ps to deny it, and the words wouldn't come.

Jared knew her silence was the only answer he would get. Why can't you talk to me?" His thumbs touched the dark ircles under her eyes. "What is it? Tell me what's wrong!"

"We're a world apart." Her eyelids drifted shut, and one ear made a slow journey down her cheek.

His hands clamped her shoulders, and he shook her ently. "You talk in riddles! Does it matter if I'm rich and ou're not? That I'm a *haole* and you're Hawaiian? This is e twentieth century! Are you ashamed of who you are? shamed of me?"

"Never!"

"Then what is it?"

When she opened her eyes, they were bright with tears. Shame has nothing to do with this. But there are differ-nces between us, loyalties we don't share."

"We can learn to share anything."

For a moment she heard his words as a promise. If she asked him to help the homesteaders, he might, as a gift to her. But even if he did, would that change anything? The homesteaders would be safe, but she would be committed to a man who had only helped them to please her. How many other favors would he do? How many times would she have to ask? How often would they look at the same situation and have two different visions? Love, lasting love, meant sharing a vision.

For the first time she understood that more than a royal tradition had kept the high mountain chief from the lowborn village maiden.

Jared saw he was losing her. "We already share so much," he said, lowering his mouth to hers.

Even as she told herself it wasn't enough, Glory succumbed to the heat of his kiss. If she couldn't have all of him forever, then she would have this much now.

Jared felt her trembling in his arms. She was wet and probably cold, but he knew the trembling came from a place deeper inside her. Glory wanted him—of that he was sure. She wanted more, too, something she wouldn't ask for, something he couldn't give her unless he understood. But she wasn't going to help him find out what it was. She had closed part of herself to him.

And suddenly he knew that if he couldn't have all of her he didn't want this. His arms dropped to his sides, and he lifted his head, stepping away. Glory made a small sound of protest, moving toward him, but he held her away. "Go back to the house," he said.

She looked at him with mute appeal. He read the truth in her eyes. He could have her here, now, if he met her even halfway. And after she'd given herself to him, he might even be able to persuade her to tell him what was wrong. But he didn't want her that way. Patsy had once been a fire in his blood. But Glory was more. She was a fire in his soul. He could not compromise her.

"Go back to the house and get some sleep." He turned away from her, staring across the darkness of the gazebo.

"Jared..."

"Yes, I want you," he said harshly. "But more than just your body, *healoha*. Do you understand what I'm saying?"

She understood only too well.

The night was silent except for the call of an owl somewhere at the edge of the silver oak grove. When Jared could stand the silence no longer, he turned. There was nothing but darkness where Glory had been.

When the knock sounded on Glory's door early the next morning, she wasn't surprised. She had wondered how long it would take Toby to track her down for a heart-to-heart talk. Toby was nobody's fool.

Given a choice, Glory would have preferred swimming to Niihau and back again to discussing Jared with anyone. She hoped she could make Toby understand that.

She padded to the door in her nightgown, opening it wide. "Come in... Patsy."

The woman standing on the other side of the threshold was dressed like a high-fashion model. Her green linen dress cost more than everything in Glory's wardrobe put together. The pearls setting off the rich hue of her smooth skin were real. Her hair was drawn back in two picture-perfect loops to fall precisely halfway down her back, and her makeup was subtle enough that Glory knew Patsy had spent a good part of the past hour on it.

Glory could have spent the same amount of time, the same amount of money on herself, and the result would never have been so perfect. Patsy had passed the line from lovely island girl to international beauty. Along the path she had garnered a hard sophistication that Glory knew she would never match, nor want to.

Patsy walked into the room. Glory watched her examine it curiously. "I've been all over Wehilani," Patsy said, "but never in the servants' quarters."

"I'm afraid you're still not there," Glory murmured shutting the door. "There is no such thing. The staff live in different places. Some in the house, some on the grounds."

"There was no one up on that horrid third floor with me."

Glory was surprised Patsy didn't try to pretend that Jared had been there with her. "I'm sorry we didn't have a better place for you. But you weren't expected."

Patsy shrugged. "Really, I'm just surprised that Jared didn't send me back down the mountain on a mule or something. I was prepared for anything."

She sounded so philosophical that Glory didn't know how to answer.

Patsy didn't seem to notice anyway. She had stopped at a drawing Glory had tacked up on the wall. It was the last of the sketches of Lono Moku, the woman in the moon, that Glory had shown Jared. It was there to remind her where she was headed when she tried to translate the charcoal sketch into acrylics as she had with the others.

"Did you do this?" Patsy asked.

"I did. Miss Hightower, why are you here?"

Patsy didn't turn. "Call me Patsy. You know, this is very good. *Very* good. I can't tell you why, but I can tell you it is. I'm told I have a good eye for art." She cocked her head seemingly absorbed. "I liked to draw as a child. I remember that until I was twelve or so I drew on everything with an inch of blank space."

Despite herself Glory was intrigued. Patsy sounded almost wistful. "What happened when you were twelve?"

Patsy laughed. "I started to develop. There wasn't much time for anything after that. I suppose I realized the fastest way out of the house was to forget about drawing and concentrate on flirting."

There was a lot Patsy hadn't said, but Glory didn't need to have the rest of the story filled in. She was just surprised that Patsy had been so revealing about her childhood, and she was curious. "Why *are* you here, Patsy?"

"May I sit down?"

Glory nodded, and Patsy seated herself on the unmade ed. Glory joined her. She had a sudden flashback to all the mes she and Peggy had sat just this way, exchanging condences. This situation seemed to get more bizarre by the cond.

"I learned long ago not to waste my time chasing rainows," Patsy said, smoothing her skirt over her knees. You can help me."

"How?"

"Was Jared putting on an act to get back at me last night? r is he really in love with you?"

Glory had expected this from the moment she had seen atsy standing in her doorway. "I don't think that's any of our business."

"Sure it is. If he's in love with you, I'm not going to beg ared to let me stay. If it's an act, I'll try to convince him. I an be very convincing."

Glory had no doubt that was true—with other men. You're saying that you'd leave if you thought Jared really ved me?" She couldn't help her next question. "Why?"

Patsy examined one of her beautifully manicured fingerails and clicked her tongue disapprovingly as if she had ound a microscopic flaw. "Jared's one of those men who'll nly love once. And he's just *full* of honor. I know when to ut my losses."

"Why did you come here, then?"

Patsy polished the suspect nail on her skirt. "Well, I hought I still had a shot at making Jared fall in love with e. I know he didn't think much of me when he broke our ngagement, but I'd hoped he'd begun to miss me."

Glory considered everything Patsy had said. The other oman was oddly pathetic. She was approaching the most otentially important relationship in her life as if she were aking her second bid at a livestock auction. Glory deided to level with her. "I'll be honest with you, if you'll be onest with me."

Patsy looked up and smiled. "Terms? I suppose I can go or that. You first."

"Jared loves me," Glory said simply.

Patsy nodded, no change of expression. "Uh-huh. Wel I guessed as much. I suppose that's that."

"Do you love him?"

Patsy hesitated as if she were truly trying to decide. The she shook her head. "I don't know."

"That's not fair. I was honest with you."

Patsy stood. "Sorry, but I'm being both fair and hones *keiki*."

Glory ignored Patsy's reference to her as a child. Next t Patsy, she was, and both of them knew it. "How can yo not know if you love Jared?"

"Because I've never thought about it." Patsy gaze around the room once more, her eyes stopping at the sketch "You know, if you're smart, you'll strike while the iron hot. Jared looked at you last night as if he wanted to hav you for breakfast, lunch and dinner. Don't play it too clos to the vest."

Instead of taking offense, Glory had the absurd urge t weep. She fought it down, knowing Patsy wouldn't appr ciate or understand her tears. "You're going home?"

"There's a man who invited me to dinner tonight. H doesn't hold a candle to Jared, but then—" Patsy opene the door "—few men do."

Glory listened to the soft click that meant Patsy was gon She felt a mixture of emotions, but none greater than sa ness that such a beautiful woman was asking for so little i her life.

For the next few hours the scene with Patsy still playe and replayed in Glory's mind. It was with her when a p litely insistent Jared asked her to join him and his guests fo breakfast in the huge dining room. It was with her lat when she took care of the one hundred and one details fo the luau that night.

Another scene played in her head, too. She felt the Weh lani mist on her skin and Jared's lips on hers. She remen

ered the words "I love you," and the hurt in his eyes when he hadn't been able to say them, too.

As she rushed from chore to chore, supervising the placement of the *kalua* pig in the pit that had been dug for it, sorting through the leis that Dave had brought from Lihue as gifts for the guests, tasting and commenting on Lucy's dishes for the feast, she searched for a way to show Jared what she felt.

When she came out of the shower, wearing only a silk kimono to dress for the party, the answer was right in front of her.

Centered on her bed was the most beautiful *haku hei*, or traditional head lei, that she had ever seen. In the customary manner, ferns, berries and a variety of leaves and flowers had been stitched painstakingly to a dried banana leaf to be tied around her head.

Glory looked up and found Toby standing in the doorway. "It's a gift from Lani," an unsmiling Toby explained. Lani, Toby's half sister, was an ethereal fairy child who more resembled Glory, who was her cousin, than anyone else in the family. The two had always had a special bond.

"It's the most beautiful one I've ever seen."

"Did you think I was going to force you to talk to me, Glory?"

Glory didn't pretend not to understand. She had skillfully avoided Toby all day, and Toby knew it. "I love you too much to tell you to mind your own business," she answered.

"When you love someone, you can tell them anything."

Glory knew Toby was talking about more than their relationship. Toby was also talking about Jared. "Sometimes talk is cheap."

Toby nodded. "And sometimes you cheapen silence when there are words screaming to be heard."

"Words can't solve this, Toby. I wish they could."

Toby waited, but Glory couldn't say any more. "Give him a chance," Toby said finally. "Give yourself a chance." She turned and left, pulling the door closed behind her.

Glory thought about Toby's visit as she dressed. There were no words to explain her emotions and her decision about the homesteaders to Jared. But she could show him. Tonight, her last night at Wehilani, she would show Jared how different they were. She would not be his estate manager tonight. She would be the woman she truly was.

Jared listened to the pleased murmur of his guests as the two young Hawaiian men who had been hired to roast the *kalua* pig ran along the edges of the estate grounds, lighting the torches that outlined the meticulously groomed gardens where the luau was being held.

"You've outdone yourself, Jared."

Jared turned to give a cursory smile to Samuel Givens and his wife, friends from New York who, after twenty-four hours on the island, had already vowed never to return to the mainland again. "I didn't do a thing," Jared admitted. "Glory did it all."

"Well, you told me she was an exceptional young woman."

Myra Givens, fiftyish and drooling over the two handsome young runners, took time from staring to point toward the house. "Did you say exceptional?"

Jared turned. Glory was coming toward them, carrying leis for all the guests. He had never seen anyone as stunningly beautiful in his life. She wore a pareu of brilliant blues, reds and purples, tied just above her breasts. As she moved it opened gracefully at the knee, revealing flower circlets around each ankle. She wore two multicolored leis on her bare shoulders, and a circlet of ferns and flowers like a crown over her forehead and hair, which fell wild and free to her hips.

Until that moment he hadn't known what it meant to need someone as much as the air he breathed. He understood now, and with his understanding came desolation.

"Mr. and Mrs. Givens, are you enjoying yourselves?" Glory asked, focusing on the guests because she didn't dare to look at Jared. She slipped a lei over each of their heads and kissed their cheeks.

"More now than I was a moment ago," Samuel said.

"Dear, just arrange an introduction to either one of those luscious young men and I'll leave you here to flirt," Myra crooned.

Glory laughed lightly. "Will you let me know if you need anything tonight?"

"Actually, Samuel needs something right now," Jared said.

Glory was forced to turn to him. He was resplendent in a black-and-turquoise aloha shirt that set off his dark good looks perfectly. Her heart beat faster, but she held her head high. She *would* get through this night. "What can I help with?" she asked politely.

"Samuel would like to see your drawings."

For a moment Glory wasn't sure she had heard Jared correctly. "Drawings?"

"I own a publishing company in New York," Samuel explained. "When Jared called me last week and asked me to come this weekend, he told me about your book. We have a well-established children's division at Givens Press. He thought I might be interested."

"You came here because of my book?"

Samuel gave a half smile. "I came because of the party. Your book makes the trip a tax write-off."

"Samuel's favors only extend so far," Jared said, taking Glory's arm. "So let's not strain his patience. Tell him he can see the sketches later tonight."

Glory murmured her permission. She knew she was being railroaded. She wanted to protest, and yet, wasn't this what she had worked for? Even though she hadn't expected or even hoped that her chance to have her work examined would come so soon, it still had.

Because of Jared. She shut her eyes for a moment as she realized that he had planned this party for her. It had been his way of persuading Samuel Givens to see her work.

The Givenses had moved away, and Glory was left alone with Jared. She felt his hand leave her arm, and she opened her eyes. He was watching her. "Are you angry?" he asked.

She shook her head. "Moved."

"There's nothing I wouldn't do for you, *healoha*."

Silently she pleaded with him to understand and forgive her. "I have to check on your other guests. It will be time to take out the pig in a few minutes."

"When are you going to talk to me?"

"Tonight. Tonight I'll tell you everything. When I do please listen."

He was frowning. "Do we have to wait?"

"There's only one way for me to explain." She shook her head when he would have asked more and started toward a group of his guests. She would never really be able to explain to Jared. She just hoped that someday, when he learned about the homesteaders, he would remember her dance and understand.

"Glory?"

She didn't want to turn back, but neither could she ignore him.

"I should have a lei, too."

She stared at the flowers looped over her arm. He was beside her again before she looked up.

In the torchlight, his face was a study in contrast. Dark touched with light, sadness touched with hope, and love...love as perfect and pure as anything she had ever seen.

Glory slipped a lei off her arm and bent toward him to slip it over his head. "Aloha," she said, never having meant the word quite this way before. She kissed him lightly on the lips, then turned toward the other guests before he could speak again.

Jared let her go only because he knew there was no way to stop her.

The sky was dark when one of the two young Hawaiian men blew a conch shell to summon the guests to dinner. Small round tables bedecked with snowy tablecloths and flower leis sat in a semicircle around a stage that Rolfe and One Leg had built for the evening's entertainment. The Hawaiian dishes for the feast—*kalua* pig; *laulau* or ti leaves stuffed with pork; salt fish; bananas; sweet potatoes; and taro shoots; chicken luau; *pipikaula* or jerked beef; and *lomi lomi salmon*—had been supplemented with some of Lucy's Oriental specialties and several all-American standbys. Guests already properly mellow after two rounds of Paradox's lethal *mai tai*s heaped their plates to the music of two slack key guitars and the sensuous vocalization of a large muumuu-clad Hawaiian woman who reminded Glory of her mother.

The night was perfect. The rain had cleared that morning, and now the moon shone as if it had never been veiled by clouds. Torches and discreet electrical supplements gave the wide expanse of lawn and garden an otherworldly glow. Insects sang their own nocturnes in tune with the vocalist, and the fragrance of flowers perfumed the air.

Glory felt the beauty of the Wehilani night like a pain inside her. After only a few bites, she excused herself.

Toby, carrying Nicky, caught up with her just as she entered the house. "Glory?"

"I'm part of the entertainment tonight. I've got to change."

"Do you need help?"

"No one can help me." Glory gave her friend a wan smile. "Go back to the party, Toby. This will be over soon."

Toby wanted to say more. It was written all over her face. She didn't, though. She just watched Glory disappear down the hallway. Then, shaking her head, she went back outside.

In her room, Glory changed into the outfit she had decided to wear. Hurriedly she tucked a strapless, gathered tunic of white cotton into a full blue gathered skirt. At home she had a more complex, traditional hula costume, but this one was authentic enough—authentic if you were talking about postmissionary Hawaii. Earlier that day she had braided an open lei of myrtle and fern fronds, which resembled the maile lei she had made for Jared at the waterfall, and now she draped it over her shoulders where it fell to her waist.

She was ready.

She wondered what Jared would think, and if he would understand. She could think of no clearer way to show him what stood between them than to dance the story of her ancestors.

The guests were finished with dinner by the time she returned to the gardens. The band was teaching them a Hawaiian song, and everyone was singing enthusiastically. Slack key music was cheerful and open, with no minor chords or blue notes to spoil the notion that everything in paradise was perfect. Glory stood off to the side of the stage, out of the lights until the song ended. Then she signaled the muumuu-clad vocalist that she had arrived.

The woman wasted no time in introducing her. Glory listened to the short explanation. The band usually didn't have the chance to delve into history, entertaining instead with songs authentic to the recent past. Tonight, however, they had the honor of playing for a dancer who would take them further back into Hawaii's heritage. The instruments they would be playing—the *ipu*, a large gourd, the *pahue*, a drum made of a hollowed coconut tree log, and the *uliuli*, decorated gourds filled with shells—had been used in Hawaiian music long before the ukelele, steel guitar or slack key guitar had been heard in the islands.

The band moved to the side of the platform, gathering their instruments before they sat down on the edge. Glory moved into the spotlight. There was a wave of spirited applause.

She smiled a little although she didn't feel like it and held up her hands for silence.

"When we planned this luau," she began, "I asked the band to bring their traditional instruments. I thought I would do one of our dances for you so you might see there's more to the music and stories of the Hawaiian people than pretty songs about little grass shacks and tiny bubbles."

She waited until the good-natured laughter died down. "Tonight, I want to go even further, though. I want to tell you about these mountains and this island. I want you to feel what happened here. Once these mountains and valleys held villages of people who, just as we're doing tonight, celebrated with feasting and song."

She stepped forward to the edge of the stage so that she could see everyone as she talked. "Did you know that the hula began here, on Kauai?" She whirled and pointed toward the mountains to her left. "There. At Haena, on the Na Pali coast. That's where the goddess of the hula, Laka, had her *heiau*. Her temple. That's where she taught my ancestors. The ruins can still be seen. It is a sacred place."

She caught Jared's eye, although she had tried to avoid looking at him. For a moment she faltered; then she went on. "Training in the hula was a supreme honor. At first only men were allowed to participate. Later the honor passed to women, too. Each movement and motion was taught over and over until it was mastered." She swung her hand over her head gracefully. "Motions like these show the sun, the heavens or creation." She thrust her hand forward at shoulder level. "This might tell of a thrown spear or a club." She bounced her knee. "This could signify billowing waves, riding a horse or a turbulent canoe ride."

She straightened, dropping her arms to her sides. "The hula began as strictly a religious expression. It changed and grew into the total panorama of Hawaiian history and myth."

The audience was silent, caught up in her story. Glory turned so that now she was facing Jared. The rest of what she had to say, she said to him.

"This island, like the others in the chain, once belonged to the Hawaiian people. Within forty years of the advent of the first Caucasians to the island, fifty percent of the native people were dead of introduced diseases. Trade offered little to those who survived. The forests were stripped of valuable sandalwood by greedy native chiefs at the expense of the agricultural practices that had sustained them for centuries. Island men pursued whaling, further diminishing the numbers needed to grow food.

"There were attempts at reform. A land act offered hope for all islanders who had never, in the old tradition, owned land before. But because they had no understanding of the law, most Hawaiians lost what they were given because they neglected to register titles, or they sold their land to foreigners." Glory saw Jared's frown. She wondered if he was beginning to understand.

"Now," she continued, softer, "only one percent of the people of Hawaii are full-blooded Hawaiians. Many more are like me, islanders of mixed blood who must study the old Hawaiian ways in books and in classes. Many of us own not one inch of the islands that were ours for centuries. As tourism expands, many Hawaiian people are driven from their homes. Paradise is lost to them forever."

She was too far from Jared to see exactly how her words had affected him, but his frown seemed to be permanent now. She went on before she had a chance to change her mind.

"These are the ways of change. Tonight I would like to dance for you and show you the way things once were. The Polynesian people have a proud heritage. We were explorers, seafarers who dared long ocean voyages in double-hulled canoes long before Christopher Columbus roamed the seas. This chant is about the first settlers, now believed to be the Marquesans, who landed on this island and settled it, possibly as early as, or even earlier than, the sixth century A.D."

Glory stepped back to the center of the stage and waited. She had chosen this group of musicians because they knew many of the traditional chants, too. There had been no time for practice. She only hoped that together they could show the audience how the mountains of Kauai had once rung with song and prayer, and with tradition.

Jared watched her stand still and proud, her head held high, her eyes fierce. He could no more fathom what had caused this outburst in the guise of a history lesson than he could fathom why she refused to admit what she felt for him. He knew only that her words had been aimed at him.

The vocalist began a haunting chant in the Hawaiian language. Jared had seen many traditional hulas in his years in the islands, but he had never seen a dancer to equal Glory. She began to move, slowly at first, but accelerating as the tempo of the chant increased. The musicians were playing their instruments, adding a throbbing rhythm to the music of the chant. Glory snapped her hips and stamped her feet, throwing her body to one side as she moved her arms to the other.

There was nothing of the graceful hotel-luau love songs in her performance. This was elemental and primitive. She moved faster, her hips and her feet beating a rhythm as old as time. Her hands spoke, telling the story of a voyage into destiny, of the sighting of land, of the promise for tomorrow.

This was not the serene, unflappable estate manager. This was a woman whose passions were as large and untamed as the islands she loved. He felt something akin to panic rising inside him. He could love this Glory, too. There was no part of her that he didn't want. But the dance, and the fierce, haughty pride in her bearing, told him that she didn't want him. She was someone he could never reach again. She had looked at the differences between them, and she believed them to be as wide as the ocean her ancestors had navigated to come to this place.

And he didn't understand why.

There was a break in the chant, and she repeated several lines in Hawaiian before she went on to a different part of the story. He watched, stricken with the savage desire to make her his, to turn her passion into something that shone for him alone. Even as he felt her slipping away from him, he wanted her more.

The dance finally ended. She bent in a graceful bow, her hair tumbling over her shoulders to the ground in front of her, her hands reaching...reaching. But not for him. Jared knew she had danced to say goodbye.

He wasn't going to let her get away with it.

Glory straightened. Jared's guests were applauding wildly. For a moment she couldn't see past the lights at the edge of the platform. Then she saw Jared striding toward her.

He was almost to the platform when a woman materialized out of the shadows. She was old, and she carried a baby on her hip. She reached Glory before Jared did.

Glory stared at the woman; then, as if she had just awakened in the midst of a nightmare only to find that it was real, she reached out and touched the woman's arm. "Kapua?"

Kapua must have journeyed from the village in the secret valley on foot. But even the miles on an overgrown mountain path hadn't dimmed the dignity in her bearing. Her voice quavered with exhaustion, but she didn't falter. "Sara is gravely ill. If we don't get her down the mountain to the hospital, I don't know if she will live." She paused. "I promised you I would come. But I would have come, anyway. I am an old woman, and there is nothing I can do now except beg for help and mercy."

"Glory?"

Glory turned. Jared's question had been nothing less than a command. She knew the time for evasion had passed, and, oddly, she was grateful. "Kapua lives with her two sons and their families on Wehilani land," she said softly so that the guests wouldn't overhear. "They've been squatting in a valley bordering state land to the west of here because they had no place else to go. One of Kapua's daughters-in-law, the mother of this child, is very ill. She needs medical care tonight."

It took only moments for Glory's words to sink in, moments more before Jared realized she had known about this for some time and hadn't told him.

"And were you ever going to tell me about them?" he asked at last, forcing all emotion from his voice.

She flinched, but she told him the truth. "No. I wasn't."

Jared stripped Glory's soul bare with one searing look. He saw her doubts, her fears, her lack of trust—and, most of all, her lies. Then he turned his back to her, facing

Kapua. "One of my guests is a doctor. He can examine your daughter-in-law. Can you ride a horse?"

Kapua nodded.

"Then we'll go by horseback. I'll take a radio with us. If we have to, we'll fly her out of here tonight. I just hope we won't be too late." He turned and strode toward John Clemens's table to begin enlisting help.

"I'll take the baby," Glory whispered, holding out her arms.

Kapua kissed her granddaughter's head, then handed her to Glory. "I didn't know what waited for me here. Now I know. Jared Farrell is the man you said he was."

"Yes." Glory rested her cheek on the baby's hair and cuddled her close. "And now he is lost to me forever."

Chapter Eleven

During the five years of her management, the Aikane Hotel had taken on much of Tony's personality. It was a cheerful, friendly place, always slightly out of step with reality. Most of the Aikane guests resided there year-round, and those few suites that were rented for shorter periods had waiting lists as long as the coast road leading back to the bright lights of Waikiki.

In her week back home, Glory hadn't visited the Aikane. She had many friends there from the years when she had helped Toby manage the hotel, but she hadn't wanted to face their questions. She had, as her mother put it, tried to force away her sorrow by pretending it didn't exist. In her usual no-nonsense manner, Nola had given her opinion of Glory's attempt. *"Lolo!"* Stupid.

On her eighth day at home, Glory admitted that her mother was right. She could no longer pretend to pick up the pieces of her life and go on as before. Nothing would ever be the same again. She had fallen in love, and she had destroyed her own chances for a happily-ever-after. Perhaps she had done what she believed was best, but that didn't hange the desolation she felt. She had to talk to someone, nd the logical someone was Toby.

Now Glory stood outside the Aikane, gazing at the newly ainted pink concrete walls. She was sure there was no pink uite like it anywhere else in the world. Glory wondered if ie painters had resorted to sunglasses as they worked. Nola ad reported that Toby had just looked at the total effect hen the painting was finished, shrugged and said, "It will ide."

In about two thousand years.

Glory caught sight of Peggy sprinting from the lobby to-ard one of the guest suites. Peggy's chestnut curls were a ild tumble, and she had twisted her orange-flowered uumuu around the fingers of one hand so that she ouldn't trip. She waved but didn't stop. Peggy had al-eady given Glory her unsolicited opinion, just as their iother had. She wasn't one to waste words, either.

Inside, Glory went straight to Toby's office. She hadn't een her friend since the night of the Wehilani luau. The etails of that night remained hazy in her mind. Toby had iken Sara's baby and cared for her. The rest of the staff had een to the guests. Jared and John Clemens had immedi-tely taken Kapua to the stables, stopping only for John's lack bag, a two-way radio and the faultlessly equipped first id kit that Jared kept for emergencies.

It was the last Glory had seen of Jared. He hadn't spo-en to her before he left, and she hadn't waited for him to ome back. She had spent a sleepless night tormenting her-elf with what she could have done differently. In the iorning she had been on the second helicopter off the iountain. First Dave had flown into the hidden valley at awn to carry Sara, Kapua and Jared to the hospital in Li-ue. He had assured Glory that John Clemens, who was ringing the horses back, had every confidence that with roper care, Sara, who was suffering from pneumonia, ould recover. Jared, he reported, had stayed in Lihue to take care of some business."

There had been no word from Wehilani since she ha
come home. There had been one brief phone call from Ne
York, though. Samuel Givens liked her rendering of th
legend of Lono Moku and wanted to see more. When sh
had asked who had shown him her work, he hadn't an
swered directly. He had only said that in her hurry to leav
Wehilani, she had left one sketch behind, tacked to he
bedroom wall. Glory had promised him that someday sh
would mail him the rest. And she would, if she was ever abl
to look at the drawings without thinking of Jared.

Now Glory wondered how Toby would greet her. Glor
had refused her friend's help when she had needed it most
She had been sure no one could help her, and she ha
wanted to spare Toby the truth. Now she knew she ha
shouldered a burden too heavy to manage alone. In th
process she had surely hurt the woman who was more siste
than friend, more friend than employer. She had hurt Toby
She had hurt Jared.

Most of all, she had hurt herself.

The door opened before she even had a chance to knock

"The door won't open by itself," Toby said from th
other side of the threshold. She chewed her bottom lip an
frowned before she spoke again. "Unless I'd left it ajar, o
course. Then it *could* blow open. But there's not really an
wind in the hallway, unless someone leaves a door open i
the lobby. People sometimes do that on hot days."

Glory went into her friend's arms for a hug. Toby onl
babbled when she felt strongly about something. Glor
knew that she'd been forgiven and Toby was trying to te
her so. It was a long time before she stepped back, and whe
she did, her eyes were wet. "I thought you might be angr
at me."

"Of course not. You're angry enough at yourself for bot
of us, aren't you?"

Glory marveled at the way that Toby—who sometime
seemed oblivious to the world around her—could always cu
right to the heart of anything that was important. "May
come in?"

Toby stepped back. Once inside, Glory seated herself on e floral-upholstered rattan love seat that looked out into e gardens surrounding the Aikane pool. Toby joined her.

"If you came to ask for your old job back, the answer is ."

Glory smiled wanly. "I didn't. Besides, I know Peggy's ing a good job."

"She is, but that's not the reason. You've outgrown this, d I don't want you trying to squeeze yourself back in."

"I don't fit anywhere anymore."

"You fit at Wehilani."

"Least of all there."

"I doubt that Jared would agree."

Glory gave a harsh laugh. "Does Jared want or need a oman who lies to him?"

"Certainly not. Especially one who lies because she esn't trust him."

Toby's words sank in slowly, and so did the pain that ac-mpanied them. Glory couldn't look at her friend. "I did hat I thought I had to do."

"Once upon a time, so did Cole," Toby answered. "I'm ing to tell you something now that I've never told anyone fore."

Glory wasn't sure she wanted to listen. "Nothing anyone n say is going to change what happened."

Toby ignored her. "Do you remember when I went to oston to search for Cole?"

Glory remembered it well. Toby had met Cole when she s swimming at the beach bordering a nearby estate. In ual Toby style, she had climbed over the iron gate to have cess to the ocean, arguing blithely that all beaches in Ha-aii were public to the high-water mark. Cole hadn't ap-eciated her argument. He had come to Hawaii for privacy, d privacy was one thing Toby didn't respect.

Their relationship had been an up-and-down affair. Toby d believed Cole to be the new estate caretaker, not the under of a burgeoning computer company. He had also en the only suspect in the murder of his estranged wife.

Against his will, he had fallen hopelessly in love with Tob
knowing, all the while, that he would be called back
Boston for trial, and that his chance of being convicted w
excellent.

When the call finally came, Cole went, with no explan
tion to Toby. He simply disappeared, leaving her fran
with worry and grief. When someone at the Aikane fina
connected the Cole Channing they had all known with
newspaper story about Nicholas Chandler III, suspect
murderer, Toby had been as shocked as everyone else. S
had also been stoutly loyal, flying immediately to Boston
find Cole and assure him that she believed in him.

She had come back devastated. No one at the Aikane ha
ever been told exactly what had passed in Boston. They on
knew that it was weeks before Toby could hold up her he
again. And it was only after Cole's innocence was esta
lished and he returned for her that Toby once again
gained her optimism and spirit.

"You don't have to tell me your secrets," Glory began

Toby held up her hand to stop her. "The day I flew
Boston, I was sure that just seeing Cole would solve eve
thing. I loved him. He loved me. What could be easier?
I had to do was tell him that I knew he hadn't killed his wi
and everything would be all right. Only it wasn't."

Toby got up, crossing her arms in front of her as s
walked to the window. "Funny, this still hurts."

"Toby—"

"It took me hours to track Cole down. I never would ha
except I found a cab driver who wanted to play James Bon
We pulled up at this elegant brownstone, well past ni
o'clock. I hadn't eaten for hours, or slept for a whole da
And I was so scared. I stuck my chin in the air and march
in to see Cole."

She paused as if the next words were the hardest to sa
"Except that Cole didn't want to see me. When he ca
downstairs he was so cold. He said he'd left without telli
me because women always make such a fuss when men a
done with them. He told me he hadn't meant it when he to

e he loved me. At first I believed he was just trying to keep e from getting hurt by everything that was happening to m. But then he added the clincher. He told me to look ound. I wouldn't fit into his life, he said, and it should be rfectly obvious why. I had been a diversion, that was all. e offered to pay my way back to Honolulu, but he warned e it was all I'd ever get from him."

Glory let out the breath she hadn't even realized she was lding. "How could he have?"

Toby turned. "Cole was doing what he thought was best r me. He lied because he didn't want me to wait for him. e was sure he was going to be sent to prison, probably for e. He knew the only way I'd ever forget him was if I be-ved he'd never loved me. He thought a lie was best. But was so wrong. It almost killed me."

Glory felt tears sting her eyes. "Yet you trust him now. I ow you do."

Toby nodded. "I trust him because I know he'll never lie me again. No matter how painful the truth may be, we ve to be truthful. Lies almost destroyed us both."

Glory didn't need coaxing to see that Toby was trying to ow the parallels between what had happened to her and lory's relationship with Jared. "I lied for the homestead-s," she protested. "Not to protect Jared."

"You didn't tell Jared the truth because you didn't trust m," Toby countered. "Just like Cole didn't trust me. He ought our love was something I could just get over, like e flu. Cole didn't understand that it could have sustained both, even if he *had* been sent to prison. You didn't be-ve that you and Jared could work out your differences. u didn't believe your love was strong enough." Toby used before she added the clincher. "Maybe you were ght."

"That's not true!" Glory stood, too. "I love him more an I ever thought possible. It tore me apart to lie to red!"

"Which Jared do you love? The one you had to keep th
truth from? That's not love! That's fear. They don't g
hand in hand."

Glory blinked back tears. Her voice wavered. "How ca
you stand there and tell me what I feel?"

"Because I stood where you're standing once and won
dered if I could ever trust Cole again. He sent me a key t
the estate after the trial was over to let me know he'd com
back. I stood in that very spot and wondered if I had th
courage to use it, to find out how strong our love still was

Toby walked over to her desk and took a key from a chin
dish on its polished mahogany surface. "This won't fit th
doors at Wehilani, Glory, but I want you to have it anywa
It's the key Cole sent me that day. Maybe it will give you th
courage you need, too." She placed the key in Glory's hand
closing her fingers over it.

"Jared will never forgive me."

"You still don't trust him, do you?"

There was no other explanation. Glory realized that Tob
was right. Trust was still at the heart of everything, after al
She hadn't trusted Jared enough to tell him about th
homesteaders. Now she didn't trust him to forgive her.

She had loved Jared. She still loved him. But she ha
never really given him a chance to show her what kind
man he was. She had guessed his reactions and acted a
cordingly. She had prejudged him because he was rich an
because his ancestors had come to the islands in a differe
way and century than hers.

She had been guilty of the same sort of prejudice of whic
she had once accused him.

"What will you lose by trusting Jared this time?" Tob
asked softly. "You say you've given him your heart a
ready."

The key felt surprisingly warm in Glory's hand. "I'll lo
my pride," she said, clutching the key tighter and holdin
it to her heart. "But perhaps that can't happen soo
enough."

* * *

The flight the next morning took twenty minutes. The taxi
le from the airport to the heliport on Poipu Beach took
enty minutes, too. Glory stood at Dave's door, wonder-
; why she hadn't had the courage to call him from Lihue.
ad she been afraid that he would gently tell her not to
ther trying to see Jared?

Whatever her reasons, she had made a mistake. Dave was
ne; Jared's helicopter was gone. Worse, on Dave's lanai
sterday's newspaper headlines peeked out from under-
ath today's. Unless the clues were misleading, Dave was
a trip somewhere, and since it was Saturday, there was a
od chance he wasn't coming back before tomorrow.

The wedding.

Glory sank down to the wooden bench beside Dave's
or. Paradox and Lucy were getting married tomorrow. In
r distress she hadn't thought about their wedding. It
uld be like Jared to plan a weekend of celebration for
em. Dave and Paradox were good friends. Dave was
obably already at Wehilani. Her timing couldn't have
en worse.

Or perhaps it couldn't have been better. She had been in-
ed to the wedding, too. No one had canceled her invita-
n. Paradox and Lucy would be pleased to see her. Maybe
red, mellowed by Paradox and Lucy's happiness, would
ar her apology and forgive her.

Maybe the goddess Pele would turn Wehilani's mountain
o a volcano and create a new tourist attraction, too.

From Dave's lanai Glory could see the mountain she
uld have to climb to ask Jared's forgiveness. Wehilani
sn't visible, but she knew it was there, out of reach, just
e way Jared surely was. By helicopter it was only minutes
ay. By foot it would take her all day and most of the eve-
ng. By horseback . . .

For the first time she was conscious of a faint whinny. She
ew that Dave kept horses, and that sometimes Jared's
ests chose to ride them to the estate rather than risk the
licopter flight. She stepped off the lanai and went around

to the side of the house. There was a small corral just p the yard beside the small barn where the horses were kept night. In that corral there was only one horse. The gray m whinnied again. Even at a distance, Glory recognized Gho

Glory thrust her hand into the pocket of her slac Toby's key reassured her. She began to close the space tween herself and the horse, increasing her pace until s was almost running. She slowed down just before the c ral and began to croon softly.

Ghost lifted her head and whinnied again. Most extra dinary of all, her silver mane was braided with flowers, a draped over her powerful shoulders was a maile lei adorn with flowers. A matching lei encircled a nearby fence pc Glory lifted it off the post with trembling hands. For a m ment she didn't recognize the tiny white blossoms scatte profusely in between scarlet lehua and maile leaves. Th as she held the lei closer, she knew. The lei maker had us the tiny naupaka blossoms, encircling the feathery leh with tiny wreaths of white.

Each blossom is only half-developed, just as the king a his true love are only half-alive because they can't be gether. Only when they are united will the naupaka gr into one perfect flower.

The naupaka was not a traditional lei flower. Someh Jared had reached out to her to tell her that they could together no matter what the obstacles that had separa them. But first the island girl had to go to the mount king. Only when they were united . . .

Glory held the lei to her chest and inhaled the sensuc fragrance of lehua and maile. Then she slipped it over head. With one foot on the bottom railing, she lifted h self over the fence.

The sun sat directly at the peak of the highest west mountain, like the brilliant star at the top of an exo Christmas tree. Glory stood holding Ghost's reins at a po where the path up the mountain diverged. The path to right led to Wehilani. To the left, just a short distance away, was the hidden valley.

She had ridden for hours because she had come to believe that somehow she and Jared could still have a future together. Now she could ride to Wehilani and ask him to forgive her. Or she could, once again, let the hidden valley stand between them.

What had Jared done about Kapua's family? He had responded with immediate assistance when he had heard about Sara's illness. But what had come afterward? What business had he stayed to take care of in Lihue that day? Had he contacted the authorities and enlisted their support to clear away the makeshift settlement? Had he filed charges?

Had Jared been touched by more than the immediate emergency? Or, once it was over, had he reverted to the man who valued privacy above everything else?

Glory knew she was still filled with doubts. Even if she didn't ride to the hidden valley to see the result of Jared's decision, the valley, and what had happened there, would still stand between them. She would have to ask Jared about the fate of the homesteaders, and by asking, he would know that she still didn't trust him.

Her decision made, she mounted Ghost again and turned left to find her answer. Ghost was rebellious. The horse, like its rider, wanted the sanctuary of Wehilani and a well-deserved rest, but Glory calmed and coaxed her until Ghost settled down to a gentle amble.

The sky was suffused with a golden glow, but the sun was no longer visible when they reached the rocks that led into the valley. Glory tied Ghost's reins to a bush, not trusting the horse to remember her training and remain if the reins were left on the ground. Glory felt compelled by more than encroaching darkness to hurry through the gash in the cliff. She wanted the moment of discovery behind her. Then, and only then, would she be able to make a decision about what to do.

She edged along the rocks until she finally came out into the open area where she and Peggy had knelt and observed the homesteaders. For a moment she couldn't bear to find out the truth. Then she stepped up to the gap leading into the valley and forced herself to look.

The valley was empty. In a moment she had eased through the rocks. She walked slowly into the clearing where once the huts had stood. There was no sign of them now, no sign they had ever existed. The goat's pen was gone, too, along with the storage shed and the camp fire circle. The fruit trees remained, but the stream irrigating the taro patch had been rerouted to its original path. The taro leaves were already beginning to wilt. Soon the land the patch had occupied would be reclaimed by native vegetation.

"Why?"

She asked the question out loud, expecting no answer. She knew that she had to find the answer inside herself. Why had Jared evicted Kapua and the others from the valley? Had their suffering meant nothing to him?

"Why do you think, Glory?"

She turned slowly. Jared's presence behind her seemed only right. For a week she had thought of no one except him. She had called up his image in her mind and heart and dreams so many times that now seeing him in the flesh seemed simply a different dimension.

She struggled with his question. He stood only yards away, but the fading light kept her from reading his expression. She didn't ask how he had found her here. She knew Toby must have alerted him. She didn't ask why he had left Ghost and the naupaka lei for her. Their message was clear. She struggled only with his question.

The answer, when it came, was from deep inside her. "Only a hard, selfish man would send these people away without helping them. You're neither hard nor selfish. You've dealt fairly with them, although I can't guess what you've done."

He moved closer until she could see the warmth in his eyes. And the relief. She saw something around his neck too, something that she hadn't noticed before. He wore a lei exactly like her own, each fringed naupaka blossom the perfect match for hers.

"I have land near Waimea that's much more suitable for homesteading than this. Kapua and her family are living there now. They'll buy it from me eventually, when they're able, at a price they can afford. Sara went home from the hospital on Wednesday. Her doctor says that, with rest and care, she'll rebuild her strength."

Glory blinked back tears. "And is there a house there? Another taro patch?"

"Two houses, small ones, but mansions to them after what they've existed in here. Ray, Sara's husband, is an excellent carpenter. He's going to start on another house in the fall. First they're planting mangoes and papayas and another taro patch." He smiled a little. "I wish we could have moved this one for them."

She took a deep breath. It turned into a sob. "Jared..."

"I know, Glory." He held out his arms to her.

She was in them in a moment, wrapping her own arms around his back. "I'm so sorry," she said. "So, so sorry."

"I'm sorry, too, *healoha*."

"You have no reason to be." She lifted her face to his. "This was my fault, my—"

His lips smothered all her protests. He kissed her hungrily, and it was a long time before he let her speak again.

"My fault," she finished through kiss-swollen lips.

"Mine, too. You told me there were differences between us. I ignored you. I should have made you talk to me, should have made you explain what differences upset you so."

"I should have told you. But I'd seen how angry you were at the backpackers. I was so afraid you'd have those people arrested. I couldn't live with that responsibility."

He held her at arm's length, and when he spoke his face was serious. "You know very little about me, and that's partially my doing. I don't share what I'm thinking." His face softened a little. "I've never had anyone to share with before."

She melted like warm caramel at the look in his eyes. "Share with me always?" she asked softly.

He answered her with his body pressed to hers and his lips searing kisses across hers. When he finally pulled away, they were both trembling. "Will you share my problems, too?"

"Those most of all," she said fervently.

His hand slid down her arm until he was holding her hand. "Come with me."

Glory let Jared lead her past the taro patch and the fruit trees to a thin border of forest overlooking the edge of the valley. Beyond them the ground tapered gently for a hundred yards, then plummeted sharply before it leveled once again, repeating the pattern. Miles in the distance the ocean glimmered, lit by the rainbow colors of sunset.

"What do you see?" he asked.

The answer was simple. "Paradise."

"The night of the luau you spoke about paradise being lost to the people of this island."

"I was trying to tell you about the homesteaders in the only way I could."

Jared gripped her hand harder. "I've lived with the dilemma of the Hawaiian people since the day so much of paradise became mine. There have been other families I've been able to help by giving away pieces of my inheritance but there are many more I'll never be able to do anything for. So much of the island is developed now. So much of nature's beauty has already been destroyed by greed and carelessness. Wehilani has never really been touched by civilization. I could turn the land over to the state of Hawaii for legal homesteading, or I can keep it as it is so that future generations can experience a piece of Kauai the way your ancestors and mine once did. Someday it could be a park or a research center or a preserve. The options are limitless."

"You talked about buying land to keep hotels from developing it. I never understood what you were really saying. You wanted to protect it, not keep it for yourself."

"It never occurred to me to tell you more." He rested his hands on her shoulders and turned her to face him. "Wehilani's a sacred trust. Will you help me decide what I should do with it?"

"I don't know what you should do," she answered honestly.

He smiled a little. "Then you see how difficult this is going to be?"

She lifted her hands to his face, stroking his cheeks with her fingertips. "I see that a decision might take a lifetime, *healoha*. But together, we have a lifetime to make it."

He pulled her closer; then, lifting his lei over her head and hers over his, he bound her to him. The naupaka blossoms nestled together, whole and perfect.

As his lips met hers, their lifetime together began.

* * * * *